ONCE
UPON A TIME
TALES

ONCE
UPON A TIME
TALES

STORIES RETOLD BY
WALLACE C. WADSWORTH

PICTURES BY
MARGARET EVANS PRICE

BARNES
&NOBLE
BOOKS
NEW YORK

This edition published by Barnes & Noble, Inc.
by arrangement with Checkerboard Press, Inc.

1995 Barnes & Noble Books

ISBN 1-56619-764-3

Printed and bound in Hong Kong

M 9 8 7 6 5 4 3 2 1

CONTENTS

INTRODUCTION

Once Upon a Time Tales unleashes readers' imaginations with splendor-filled tales of wonder, magic, and adventure. These seventeen stories are masterfully retold by Wallace C. Wadsworth and are graced with the art of Margaret Evans Price. Journey into the world of storyland where breathtaking tales await you!

All of the stories in this volume are long-time classics. One such favorite is that of tiny Tom Thumb. After being created at whim by Merlin the wizard, Tom wanders through Fairyland playing roguish tricks while displaying keen wit and charm. In the tale of "Peter Rabbit," merry laughter rings out over the good scare that the lively and thoughtless Peter has at the hands of Mr. McGregor. How lucky he is to learn that "mother knows best" at no greater cost than an unpleasant dose of camomile tea! Then, there is the miraculous manner in which the disadvantaged brother in "How the Sea Became Salt" masters his difficulties after gaining possession of a magic hand-mill. For him, it becomes the source of all good things, but for others who covet the mill solely to satisfy their greed, it only brings disaster. In addition to learning the evil of avarice, we also are given a mythological explanation for the salty sea.

This richly-varied collection also contains fine examples of noodle stories—folk stories that depict ludicrous doings of very foolish people. Two of these silly narratives are "Mr. and Mrs. Vinegar" and "Henny Penny." Witness Mr. Vinegar, a delightful and silly dunce, as his possessions diminish from cow to bagpipes, from bagpipes to gloves, from gloves to a walking cane, and from a walking cane to nothing at all. Only through Mrs. Vinegar's common sense is the Vinegar family brought back to a contented life. Henny Penny, a simpleton hen, absurdly concludes that the sky is falling once she is struck by a falling acorn. With the whole barnyard following her, she races to forewarn the country's King, making the affair twice as ridiculous.

Many more stories are included in *Once Upon a Time Tales* which are sure to delight readers of all ages. "The Three Bears," "The Pied Piper," "The Seven Wonderful Cats," "Bluebeard," and "Puss in Boots" are just a few. Good tales never grow stale or out of date—in fact, their flavor always improves with the passage of time. Enjoy this remarkable and imaginative collection that is sure to delight readers everywhere!

THE COCK, THE MOUSE, AND THE LITTLE RED HEN

There once lived together, in a neat little white house upon a pleasant hillside, a Cock and a Mouse and a Little Red Hen.

The Little Red Hen worked hard all day, keeping the little house clean and in order, cooking the food, washing the dishes, and mending the clothes. But the Cock and the Mouse were very lazy and did no work at all.

Across the valley, on another hillside, a wicked Fox had his den among some trees and big stones. He often wondered who lived in the little white house, and one day he set forth to find out.

"Goodby," he called back to Mrs. Fox and their three little foxes, who were always hungry. "Perhaps the little white house belongs to someone we can eat." And the three hungry little foxes jumped with joy at the thought.

Away the wicked Fox ran, down the long hill, over the stepping stones that crossed the creek in the valley, and then ran up the other long hill toward the little white house. As he came nearer, he slipped along behind bushes and rocks, so that nobody could see him.

At last he crept up and peeped in at the window. And there he saw the Cock and the Mouse, sitting back sleepily in their easy chairs. They were so plump and fat that they made him very hungry for them. He also saw the Little Red Hen bustling about, and though she was not at all fat, he grew hungry for her, too.

Then away from the window he slipped, and ran all the long way back to his den.

"What a wonderful dinner we shall have!" the wicked Fox said to his mate and their little ones.

"In the little white house live a Cock and a Mouse who are fat and tender, and a Little Red Hen who is not at all fat, because she works so hard. But surely she'll be tender enough for strong white teeth to eat."

"Yes, indeed," said Mrs. Fox, and the little foxes all leaped with joy at the thought.

THE LAZY COCK AND THE LAZY MOUSE

So the wicked Fox took a big bag, and a piece of string to tie it with. Then he set out to catch the Cock, the Mouse, and the Little Red Hen and bring them home for dinner.

And because the wicked Fox was so sure of getting them for dinner, Mrs. Fox and the three little foxes got everything ready to cook the Cock, the Mouse, and the Little Red Hen. They gathered firewood and kindling, and they got out their biggest, blackest pot and hung it over the fire to boil.

Again the wicked Fox ran down the hillside, across the creek on the stepping stones, and slipped up toward the little white house. He sneaked along behind bushes and rocks, and at last he crept up to the window once more, and looked in.

There were the lazy Cock and Mouse, just as before, and there also was the busy Little Red Hen, bustling about like a bright ray of sunshine.

"Who will make the fire to cook dinner with?" the Little Red Hen was asking.

"Not I," grumbled the Cock, sitting back deeper in his easy chair.

"Nor I," grumbled the fat little Mouse, stretching out lazily.

"Then I'll do it myself," said the the Little Red Hen, and she made a hot fire to cook dinner with.

"Now who will peel the potatoes for dinner?" she asked.

"Not I," grumbled the lazy Cock.

"Nor I," pouted the lazy little fat Mouse.

"Then I'll do it myself," said the Little Red Hen, and she set to work peeling the potatoes and getting the other things ready to cook for dinner.

"Now who will put the pot on to boil?" asked the Little Red Hen.

"Not I," grumbled the lazy Cock.

"Nor I," pouted the lazy little fat Mouse.

THE FOX GRABBED THE MOUSE BY HIS LONG TAIL
AND DROPPED HIM INTO THE BAG

"Then I'll do it myself," and she put the pot on to boil and cooked dinner without any help.

"Now who will eat dinner with me?" the Little Red Hen asked at last, when the dinner was all ready and on the table.

"I will!" cried the Cock.

"I will, too!" cried the fat little Mouse.

And up they both jumped and rushed to the table. There they both ate so fast and so much that the Little Red Hen didn't get her share. And when dinner was over, the Cock and the Mouse had eaten so much that all they wanted to do was to get back into their easy chairs for a long nap.

"Now who will help me clean off the table and wash the dishes?" asked the Little Red Hen.

"Not I," said the Cock, sleepily.

"Nor I," said the Mouse, yawning.

"Then I'll do it myself," and the Little Red Hen bustled about, cleaning off the table and washing the dishes.

"Who will help me sweep and dust the upstairs?" she asked, when the last dish was put away.

"Not I," grumbled the Cock.

"Nor I," squeaked the lazy Mouse.

"Then I'll do it myself," said the Little Red Hen, and up the stairs

THE FOX DROPPED THE COCK IN THE BAG
ON TOP OF THE MOUSE

3

she hurried with broom and dustcloth, leaving the Cock and the Mouse to go fast asleep in their easy chairs.

The wicked Fox smiled to himself when he saw the Little Red Hen go upstairs, and saw the lazy Cock and the lazy Mouse close their eyes in sleep.

He stepped up to the door, and knocked—rap-rap-rap!

The sound awoke the Cock and the Mouse. "I wonder who that can be!" said the Mouse.

"Open the door and see," said the lazy Cock, and closed his eyes again.

"It's probably the grocery boy, bringing us some more things to eat," said the Mouse, and he got out of his chair and went to the door. Sleepily he opened the door, but he woke up quickly enough when he saw the wicked Fox standing on the doorstep.

"Squeak! sque-e-e-eak!" he cried in great fright, and rushed for a place to hide as the Fox pushed the door open wide and walked in.

The Cock opened one eye, and when he saw the Fox he tried to fly up on top of a high cupboard.

"Cock-a-doodle-doo!" cried the Cock, and flapped his wings, but he was so fat and heavy that he couldn't fly at all!

The wicked Fox laughed as he grabbed the Mouse by his long tail and dropped him into his bag, and then grabbed the frightened Cock by his long neck and dropped him in on top of the Mouse.

The Little Red Hen upstairs heard the noise, and came running down to see what the trouble was. And as she ran down the stairs she ran right into the paws of the wicked Fox, and he popped her into the bag, too! Then he tied the mouth of the bag fast with his piece of string.

The Fox threw his heavy load up over his shoulder and started down the hill, laughing to think how easily he had caught such a good dinner for his mate and little ones.

As for the Cock, the Mouse, and the Little Red Hen, they were all so crowded together in the bag that they could hardly move. The wicked Fox shook them about so much as he walked down the rough hillside that they were very uncomfortable, and the Cock and the Mouse both began to feel sorry they had been so lazy.

"This is the end of all of us!" mourned the Cock. "I am to blame, because I was too lazy to get up and see who was at the door."

"And I am to blame because I opened the door without looking first," squeaked the Mouse, and they both began to cry.

"GOODNESS, BUT THIS IS A HEAVY LOAD!" CRIED THE FOX

"Cheer up! Cheer up!" said the Little Red Hen, as brightly as she could. "Perhaps something will turn up." She was cheerful because she had just remembered that she had her sewing box in her pocket, and believed that it might help her to get them all out of the bag.

After a while the wicked Fox reached the bottom of the long hill, and his bag was so heavy that he was tired from carrying it. So when he came to a big tree beside the creek he dropped his bag to the ground. He sat down beside it, leaned back against the tree to rest, and so tired was the wicked Fox that almost at once he fell fast asleep.

DROPPING HIS HEAVY LOAD THE FOX SAT DOWN

"Now is our chance," said the Little Red Hen, and from her sewing box she took her sharp little scissors. Snip! snip! they went, and in a moment she had made a hole big enough for the Mouse to crawl out through.

"Find a stone as big as yourself, and roll it up to the bag," the Little Red Hen told the Mouse as he crawled out.

Then snip! snip! and she made the hole big enough for the Cock to crawl out through.

"Find a stone as big as yourself," the Little Red Hen told the Cock as he slipped out, "and roll it up to the bag."

Then she herself crawled out through the hole in the bag, and started looking for a stone just as big as she herself was.

The Mouse rolled his stone up to the bag, and shoved it in through the hole. Then the Cock rolled his stone up to the bag, and shoved it also in through the hole.

By that time the Little Red Hen had found her stone and had rolled it up to the big bag, and then it, too, was shoved in through the hole.

When the Little Red Hen saw that all the stones were in the bag, she quickly took out her little sewing box once more. Then, with a

6

THE FOX CAME TO THE STEPPING STONES THAT LED ACROSS THE CREEK

big needle and some heavy thread, she sewed up the big hole so

hidden safely behind some stones and bushes near by.

The Fox picked up his bag, and

stepped from one to the other toward the other side.

Just as he came to the middle, his foot slipped and — splash! — the heavy bag fell from his shoulder into the water and sank out of sight before he could so much as bat an eye or whisk his tail.

"Oh, dear! Oh, dear!" he cried. "There goes our dinner!"

And sadly he trudged on home to his den to tell his. mate and his little ones that the Cock, the Mouse, and the Little Red Hen were now at the bottom of the creek, and that they never, never could be eaten for dinner by the Fox family.

As for the Cock, the Mouse, and the Little Red Hen, they waited until the wicked Fox had gone away, and then they ran for home just as fast as ever they could run.

And there they locked the door behind them, and sat down to catch their breath. You may be sure they were very, very thankful to be safely back in their cozy little white house once more.

"I shall never be lazy or cross again," said the Cock to the Little Red Hen. "I shall carry in the wood and I shall make the fires, and I shall do anything else you ask me to do."

"I, too," squeaked the Mouse. "The Cock and I will do the work, and you can sit in my easy chair and rest."

And so the three lived happily together ever after, and were never again bothered by the wicked Fox. For, you see, he thought the Cock, the Mouse, and the Little Red Hen were all at the bottom of the creek where he never could get them.

THE SEVEN WONDERFUL CATS

In a pleasant little house beside a wide river there once lived a little old lady whose name was Dame Wiggins of Lee. Dame Wiggins was a very worthy old soul, but she was often unhappy because she was so very lonely.

"What would I not give," she often said to herself, "to have some-one here in my little house to keep me company! Someone with learning, perhaps, who could talk to me about the things wise men have written in books. Or someone who could sing, and keep me cheered up with music. Or someone who could help me mend and sew, or even someone who would just amuse me with bright antics."

Often, when the pain in her knee troubled her, she would wonder: "What would become of me should I fall ill, with no one here to nurse me? What should I do for food, could I no longer get out to market? Oh, me! Oh, my! How very much alone I am!"

But she was not really alone, for in her little house and little barn were many, many rats and mice. Dame Wiggins of Lee, however, hated rats and mice. Instead of being glad to have their company, she longed to find a way to get rid of every one of them.

One day a neighbor was passing by, and he spied Dame Wiggins of Lee sweeping off her doorstep. "Good morning to you, good Dame Wiggins," he called. "And how are you today?"

"Very well, neighbor, and thank you," said the good Dame, "except that I'm such a lonesome old soul, and my knee hurts me terribly at times. Besides that, the rats and mice are about to eat me out of house and home."

"Aha!" said the neighbor. "Rats and mice, say you? Then I have just the thing for you. I have Seven Wonderful Cats that you may have, and they will soon make short work of all your rats and mice."

And sure enough, the very next day the neighbor sent his Seven Wonderful Cats to Dame Wiggins of Lee. They were dressed just alike, all seven of them, in little red trousers and little blue coats with big brass buttons. And the name of every one of them was Tommy!

EACH TOMMY SETTLED DOWN BY A BIG HOLE
AND WAITED FOR HIS DINNER

"Welcome, my fine cats!" Dame Wiggins of Lee cried happily, when she beheld them. "Now I shall not be lonely any more!"

"Indeed, and you shall not," said all the Tommies together, and they smiled brightly and wiggled their whiskers at her. "We hear that you have here many rats and mice, upon which we may make many good dinners."

"There are far too many of them here," said the good Dame, greatly pleased to see what fine manners the Tommies had. "Follow me, my fine cats and I will show you their holes."

So they followed her through the little house and the little barn, and she pointed out all the rat and mouse holes to them. Then each Tommy settled down by a big hole, and wiggled his whiskers fiercely, and glared with his big green eyes, and waited for his dinner to run out through the hole.

The Seven Wonderful Cats soon caught so many rats and mice that they were hungry no longer. So they went into the house, and there they curled up and went to sleep upon seven big pink pillows which Dame Wiggins had fixed for them.

Every day this fierce-whiskered crew caught rats and mice, until soon all the rats and mice were gone from the little house and the little barn of Dame Wiggins.

And at last the Seven Wonderful Cats went to Dame Wiggins and said, "Not a rat or a mouse is to be found around your little house or in your little barn. We have caught them all, or frightened them away."

"Well done, my fine cats," said Dame Wiggins of Lee. "Now I shall never be troubled by rats and mice again."

So as a reward she gave each Tommy a big saucer of cream.

"Now, my fine cats," said she, when they had lapped up the last drop, "since the rats and mice are gone, what do you wish to do?"

"Now that our work is all done," said the Seven Wonderful Cats, "we should like to go to school."

"Go to school!" cried Dame Wiggins. She was much surprised, for never before had she heard of cats going to school. "To be sure! If school you wish, to school you shall go."

So she sent them off to school, with a note to the master telling him what wonderful cats they were.

At school the Seven Wonderful Cats studied long and hard, so that they learned very fast. And soon they could read the words "milk" and "rat" and "mouse," and could spell the word "mew." The master thought he had never seen such wonderful cats, as indeed he hadn't, and he wrote a fine letter to Dame Wiggins telling her what a credit they were to her.

After learning to read and spell, the cats learned many other things, until they were very wise indeed.

And when they were not studying, they spent their playtime learning to fish. Often they sent to Dame Wiggins of Lee presents of fish which they had caught.

"What fine cats!" the good Dame would say. "Here they have sent me another fish for my dinner!"

AT SCHOOL THE CATS LEARNED TO READ AND SPELL

But though she was glad to know how well they were doing, she was also very lonely without them. That is why, when it was almost winter, she sent for them to come home.

So home they came, and came in a very strange manner. Down the river to the house of good Dame Wiggins they rowed, each one in a little rowboat.

"Oh, the dears!" said Dame Wiggins of Lee. "Did anyone ever before see such wonderful cats?"

She welcomed them home, and they spoke to her in such a wise and learned manner that the good old

11

lady was delighted. "Now that they are educated," said she, "I shall never again be without wisdom in my little house."

Then, very happy that they had learned so much in school, she ran out to market to get some good things for their supper. And when she came back she found her Seven Wonderful Cats mending the parlor carpet, each handling his needle as briskly as a bee.

"What wonderful cats they are!" she cried. "And now I shall never again be without someone to help me mend and sew." And then Dame Wiggins set to work and cooked the seven cats a fine supper.

SUCH FUNNY FALLS DID THE CATS TAKE!

The next day she went to market again, and when she came back, what do you think the Seven Wonderful Cats were doing? The river had frozen over during the night, and the seven Tommies were having a fine time skating on the ice.

So amusing did they look, and such funny falls did they take, and so happy were they, that good Dame Wiggins of Lee just sat down on the bank and laughed until she cried. "I shall never again be without someone to amuse me with bright antics!" she said, as she dried the tears of laughter from her eyes.

So all the long winter through, the Seven Wonderful Cats kept Dame Wiggins of Lee bright and happy, and she never grew lonely any more.

By and by spring came, and the Seven Wonderful Cats began to take long strolls through the fields.

In their strolls they were very careful not to disturb the little birds that were building nests. They were very well-mannered cats, indeed, and never wanted to eat little birds, as ordinary cats always do.

"My fine cats," said good Dame Wiggins one morning, "if you'll all climb into the big walnut tree, and sit there like good cats, all seven in a row, I am sure the little birds will teach you how to sing."

"OH, THE DEARS!" SAID THE DAME AS THE SEVEN WONDERFUL CATS CAME ROWING HOME

EVERY NIGHT THE SEVEN WONDERFUL CATS PLAYED AND SANG TO GOOD DAME WIGGINS OF LEE

So the Seven Wonderful Cats climbed the big walnut tree, and sat there on a limb, all seven in a row. And the meadow larks and the bluebirds and the robins and many other song birds came and gave them singing lessons, because they were such good cats.

After they had learned how to sing, they often sang to Dame Wiggins of Lee. Every evening they would sit by the fireside and sing—"Mew! Mew! Miaou! Mr-r-rrow-rr!!"—all together, just as loud as they could. And Dame Wiggins, who couldn't hear very well, always asked them to sing their song again and again. She thought it very sweet, and she praised their voices highly.

So pleased was she with their progress in music that she bought each of them a little trumpet to play on when they were tired of singing. And every night they played and sang for her until bedtime. "Ah me!" said the good Dame happily. "I shall never be without music again."

One morning, when they were out visiting the little birds, they came

14

upon a poor little sick lamb that had lost its mother.

"How sad!" said the Seven Wonderful Cats. "We must help this poor little sick lamb, and find its mother for it." So they hunted about and found a wheelbarrow. Then they put the little lamb on the wheelbarrow and wheeled it home.

Dame Wiggins was overjoyed at their kindliness. "You shall all have some sprats for your good deed!" she promised. Then she hurried away to the field to look for the little lamb's mother.

While she was away, the Seven Wonderful Cats turned down the covers and warmed the sheets and put the poor little lamb safely to bed.

The Dame could not find the old mother sheep. So she came back home. And when she saw what the Seven Wonderful Cats had done she was well pleased.

"I shall never be without a nurse, should I fall ill!" she said happily.

The next morning, when the Dame came downstairs early, she noticed that not a cat was about.

"Oh, dear! Oh, dear! Where can they be!" cried the good lady, for she didn't know what had happened to them. "Here, pussy, puss, puss!" But not a single Tommy showed himself in answer to her call.

Before long, however, there was a great fuss and commotion outside. The Dame ran to the door and looked out, and what do you think she saw?

Here came her Seven Wonderful Cats, each one riding upon the back of a sheep, and driving a whole flock of sheep before them! They had gone in search of the sheep, for they were sure that the lamb's mother must be in the flock somewhere.

"Well done, my fine cats!" cried Dame Wiggins of Lee. And she was unable to hide her joy when the little sick lamb cried "Baa-a-a!" and jumped out of bed and ran straight to its mother. The good Dame was

THE CATS PUT THE SICK LITTLE LAMB TO BED

15

EACH CAT TOOK A RIDE ON THE BACK OF A GOOSE

so happy that she cried for joy and started dancing about, in spite of her gout and the pain in her knee.

The farmer who owned the sheep soon noticed they were gone from the pasture, and came in search of them. He stepped up to the Dame's door, his dog Tray at his heels, and knocked with his crook. "Good morning, Dame Wiggins," he said, when the old lady stuck her head out of the door. "Have you seen my sheep?"

"Yes, indeed," said Dame Wiggins. "My Seven Wonderful Cats have just taken them back to their pasture," and she told him how they had found the sick lamb and had cared for it and found its mother.

"What wonderful cats!" said the farmer. "I must reward them." So when the Seven Wonderful Cats came back from taking the sheep to pasture, there was the farmer waiting for them. He had hitched up his team of horses to his wagon, and he gave them all a ride to his farmhouse.

The farmer, for their kindness, gave them a wonderful dinner of field mice and raspberry jam. And for dessert they had all the cream they could drink. They were so pleased with their dinner they decided to give him some fine music, and straightway began singing and blowing their trumpets in their very best manner.

"Very good, my fine cats," the farmer said, laughing heartily and holding his hands to his ears. "Dame Wiggins must be deaf to listen to such grand and beautiful music."

Then, before they could start another song, he led them all out into his barnyard. "Come with me," he said, "and I'll show you all my fine stock." And after him they followed, to see his fine stock.

He opened the gate to his poultry yard, the better to show them all his chickens and ducks and geese. The fowls all ran out through the open gate, and the cats were much amused.

Last of all, the big geese ran out, and as they waddled through the gate, each of the Seven Wonderful Cats jumped upon the back of a big goose to take a ride.

The geese were so frightened that they honked just as loud as they could, and ran down to the river. There they jumped into the water, and swam about and ducked the cats on their backs until the Seven Wonderful Cats were half drowned. The farmer was so amused at their antics that he laughed long and heartily.

When at last the Seven Wonderful Cats got back on shore again, they combed the water from their fur and wrung it from their clothes.

"Now, if it please you," said they to the farmer, "we must be getting home before we all catch cold."

"Very well," laughed the farmer, and put them in his big wagon again and took them home. For their kindness to his lamb, and for making him laugh so much, he gave them a big ham and many other presents.

"Oh, my fine cats, what a wonderful big ham you have!" cried Dame Wiggins of Lee when they showed her all their presents.

"Surely, I shall never want for anything so long as I have my Tommies! Now come in to supper, and sit down with me. Then after supper is over you must all take some ginger tea and go right to bed, or you will take cold. And I can't risk losing my Seven Wonderful Cats!"

ONLY THE CAT WAS LEFT FOR THE YOUNGEST SON

PUSS IN BOOTS

Once upon a time a miller died and left all he possessed to his three sons. But he had only these three things, his mill, his ass, and his cat.

The division of the property was soon made. The eldest brother took the mill. The second son received the ass. That left only the cat for the youngest, who could not be consoled for his bad luck.

"My brothers," said he, "will be able to earn a living, if they work together. But when I have eaten my cat, and made a fur collar of his skin, I shall die of hunger!"

The cat had heard all this. Now he said, "Do not worry, master. Give me a hempen sack, and have me made a pair of boots, that the brambles may not tear my feet. You shall see that you have not fared so badly."

The cat's owner did not put much faith in all this. Still, he had seen the cat do a great many clever feats. Sometimes he would hang himself by his feet, or hide himself in a bag of meal, pretending to be dead. This was only a trick to catch rats and mice. So now he did not entirely despair.

As soon as the cat had got what he asked for, he put on his fine new boots and hung the sack around his neck. Then he went off to a rabbit warren. Inside the bag he put some bran and some thistles. Then he stretched himself out, pretending to be dead, and waited for a rabbit to rummage in the bag and eat what he had put there.

Hardly had he lain down when a reckless young rabbit ran into the sack. Then Sir Cat, drawing tight the strings, had him at his mercy.

The cat now went to the King. He was shown the way to the King's audience chamber. Making a fine low bow to the King, he said, "Sire, here is a rabbit which my lord the Marquis of Carabas has bidden me bring you."

"Say 'thank you' to your master, and tell him I am much pleased," said the King.

Another time the cat hid in a wheat field. This time two partridges walked into his bag. At once he drew tight the strings, and the birds were safely caught. These he presented to the King, as he had the rabbit. The king was delighted, and gave orders that the cat should be given something good to eat.

Thus the cat kept on for two or three months. One day he learned that the King was going the next morning to drive on the banks of the mill stream with his daughter, who was the most beautiful princess in the whole world. So he said to his owner, "If you will take my advice, your fortune is made. You have only to go bathing in the stream. I will show you where."

The cat's master could not see what good could come of it. Still he did as Puss advised.

While he was enjoying his bath the King passed by. Now what did Sir Cat do, but begin to cry

with all his might, "Help! help! The most honorable Marquis of Carabas is drowning!"

The King put his royal head outside the curtains of his carriage. As soon as he recognized the cat, he commanded his royal guard to run in haste to the aid of the most honorable Marquis of Carabas.

While they were dragging the Marquis out of the water, the cat drew near the royal coach. He told the King that thieves had come and carried away all his master's clothes. Now it was really the cat himself who had hidden them.

The King ordered his Royal Wardrobe Keeper to go and fetch some of his finest garments for the most honorable Marquis.

The fine clothing set off his good looks so well the King's daughter found him exceedingly to her taste. The Marquis of Carabas had no sooner looked at her two or three times than she liked him very much indeed. The King desired him to join the royal party on its drive.

The cat went running ahead. On meeting some peasants who were mowing he said to them, "Good folk who mow, if you do not tell the King that this meadow belongs to the most honorable Marquis of Carabas, you shall be minced as fine as pie meat!"

"They all belong to the Marquis of Carabas!" they answered, and the King rejoiced at the good fortune of the Marquis. The cat kept saying the same thing to everyone he met. Even the King was amazed at the marvelous riches of the Marquis.

At last Puss reached a great castle. The owner was an Ogre. He was the richest Ogre you ever saw, for all the lands through which the king had passed really belonged to him. The cat had taken pains to find out what the Ogre could do. Now he asked if he could speak with him.

"I've been told," said Sir Cat, "that you can change yourself into any sort of animal—for instance, into a lion, or even into an elephant!"

When the King passed, he asked the mowers whose meadow they were mowing. "It belongs to the Marquis of Carabas," they all said, for they were frightened by the cat's warning.

"You have a noble inheritance," said the King to the Marquis.

"As you see, Sire," replied the Marquis, "'tis a meadow which never fails to produce abundantly."

Puss came next to some reapers. To them he said, "Good folk, if you do not tell the King that these crops belong to the Marquis of Carabas, you shall be chopped as fine as the mincemeat for a pie!"

A few moments later the King passed by that way, and wished to know to whom these crops belonged.

"That's true," said the Ogre, crossly, "and to prove it you shall see me change into a lion!"

Puss was so frightened to see a real lion in front of him that he reached the roof in the twinkling of an eye and climbed out upon the gutters for greater safety.

When Puss saw that the Ogre had changed back again, he came down from the roof. He confessed that he had had a very great fright!

"I've also been told," said Puss, that you can take the shape of the very tiniest animal; for example, a rat, or even a mouse! I'll admit that I think it quite impossible."

"Impossible!" roared the Ogre. "You shall see for yourself!" And instantly he changed into a mouse and began to run about upon the floor. No sooner did the eyes of Puss in Boots fall upon the mouse than he threw himself upon it and ate it up!

Now the King, as he passed by, noticed the mighty castle of the Ogre and wished to visit it. Puss in Boots ran to meet the royal party. "Welcome, your Majesty!" he said. "Welcome to the castle of the most honorable Marquis of Carabas!"

"How is this, Marquis?" cried the King. "This wonderful palace, too, is yours? Nothing can be lovelier than this courtyard. Let us see the inside, I pray you."

Following His Majesty, who entered first, they all went into the great hall. There they found ready a luncheon which the Ogre had ordered to be prepared for friends.

After seeing the immense wealth of the Marquis, and having drunk his health, the King said to him, "There is no one, my dear Marquis, whom I should like better as my son-in-law. It rests only with you."

The Marquis, with a low bow, accepted joyfully the honor offered him by the King.

As for Puss in Boots, he became a great lord and hunted little mice only when he wanted amusement.

BOB-WHITE AND THE FARMER MAN

Once upon a time there was a little quail whose name was Bob-White. And he had a little mate whose name was Mrs. Bob-White.

One spring day they were looking about for a good place to build their nest, and they spied a green field of wheat.

"Oh, what a lovely green wheat field!" said Mrs. Bob-White. "That will be a good place for us to build our nest."

"Yes, it is just the place," agreed Bob-White. "It will hide our nest so that no one can ever find us, for the wheat stalks will grow up tall and strong. And besides, there are always bugs and other good food to be found in wheat fields."

So Bob-White and Mrs. Bob-White built their nest in the wheat field. They built it down on the ground, and the tops of the wheat stalks grew up over it and hid it so that no one could find it except Bob-White and his little mate.

And there were so many bugs and so much other food to be found among the wheat that they were both very glad they had chosen the wheat field for their home.

Before long the nest had ten little white eggs in it. After a while longer, the shells were broken and ten little Bob-Whites were in the nest. Soon they were ready to run and play among the wheat.

Mrs. Bob-White led the little Bob-Whites about through the field every day, showing them how to find bugs and other food. Also, she taught them things which every little Bob-White must know.

She taught them what to do when there was danger near. She would give a little call, and then every little Bob-White must hide and be just as still as still could be. And while they were hiding, Mrs. Bob-White would flutter along the ground as if her wing were broken and she couldn't fly. She would flutter and hop along until she led any stranger far away from where her little ones were hidden. Then she would suddenly spring up and fly back to them.

The ten little Bob-Whites grew and grew, and soon they grew big enough so that it was time for them to learn how to fly. "Tomorrow we must start teaching our little ones how to fly," said Mrs. Bob-White one evening. "For in another week they will be big enough to take care of themselves, and they must know how to fly well."

"We must teach them right away," agreed Bob-White. "The wheat is getting ripe, and the Farmer Man will soon be cutting it. Our little ones must know how to fly before that happens, or else the mower's sharp blade may catch them as it comes through the grain."

Mrs. Bob-White grew somewhat worried when she looked at the wheat. Sure enough, it was now almost golden instead of green, and it would soon be ready to cut. "But perhaps they will not cut it right away," said she. "If it is not cut for a week yet, our little ones will know how to fly and will then be out of danger."

The very next day Bob-White and his mate started teaching the ten little Bob-Whites how to fly. The little ones learned fast, but they would not be able to fly for five days yet.

That evening Bob-White said to Mrs. Bob White: "I saw the Farmer Man and his sons at the edge of the wheat field today. The Farmer Man said that he thought they ought to begin cutting the wheat tomorrow."

"THE WHEAT IS GETTING RIPE," SAID BOB-WHITE

"Oh, dear me!" cried Mrs. Bob-White. "Whatever shall we do? Our little ones can't fly yet, and the mower's sharp blade will surely catch them among the wheat!"

"That will be all right," said Bob-White. "Don't worry, for they will not cut the wheat tomorrow."

"Well," said Mrs. Bob-White, "perhaps you're right. If it isn't cut for five days yet, our little ones will be out of danger."

And, sure enough, when the next day came the wheat was not cut, but went on ripening under the hot sun.

That day the ten little Bob-Whites were given another lesson

24

in flying, and they did so well that their father and mother were very proud. "In four days now they will be able to fly and look after themselves," said Mrs. Bob-White that evening.

"I saw the Farmer Man and his eldest son at the edge of the field today," said Bob-White. "The Farmer Man told his son to start cutting the wheat tomorrow."

"Oh, dear me!" cried Mrs. Bob-White. "Whatever shall we do? Our little ones can't fly yet, and the mower's sharp blade will surely catch them among the wheat!"

"That will be all right," said Bob-White. "Don't worry, for they will not cut the wheat tomorrow."

THE FARMER MAN TELLS HIS SON TO CUT THE WHEAT

"Well," said Mrs. Bob-White, "perhaps you're right. If it isn't cut for four days yet our little ones will know how to fly and will then be out of danger.

And, sure enough, when the next day came the wheat was not cut, but grew riper and riper under the hot sun.

That day another lesson was given to the ten little Bob-Whites. This time they learned so much that they could lift themselves off the ground with their wings and flutter along in the air for a short way. "Just think!" cried Mrs. Bob-White that evening, "in three more days they will be able to fly!"

"And none too soon," said Bob-White. "I saw the Farmer Man and his second son at the edge of the field today. The Farmer Man said that since the eldest son had to go to town today, and so hadn't cut the wheat, the second son must cut it tomorrow."

"Oh, dear me!" exclaimed Mrs. Bob-White. "Whatever shall we do? Our little ones can't fly well yet, and the mower's blade will surely catch them among the wheat!"

"Don't worry," said Bob-White. "For they will not cut the wheat tomorrow."

And, sure enough, the next day came and the second son did not cut

THE TEN LITTLE BOB-WHITES LEARN TO FLY

the wheat. He was not feeling well that morning, and did not work at all that day, so the wheat grew still riper under the hot sun.

The ten little Bob-Whites learned to fly farther than ever that day. In two days more they would be able to fly well.

That evening Bob-White said to his little mate: "I saw the Farmer Man and his youngest son at the edge of the field today. The Farmer Man was worried because the wheat was not cut today, and told his youngest son to cut it tomorrow."

"Oh, goodness me!" cried Mrs. Bob-White. "Whatever shall we do? Our little ones can't fly at all well yet, and the mower's sharp blade will surely catch them among the wheat!"

"Don't worry," said Bob-White. "They will not cut the wheat tomorrow, and in two days more our little ones can fly and will be out of danger."

Nor did the Farmer Man's youngest son cut the wheat the next day. He had a toothache, and didn't work at all that day.

26

THE HIRED MAN FELL AND STUBBED HIS TOE

The little Bob-Whites learned their lessons so well that day their parents were delighted.

"They are learning to fly very fast," said Mrs. Bob-White that evening. "And if they do as well tomorrow, when the wheat is cut they will be in no danger from the mower's sharp blade, for then they will all ten of them be able to fly safely away."

"I saw the Farmer Man and his hired man at the edge of the field today," said Bob-White. "The Farmer Man is determined that the wheat shall be cut tomorrow, and he told his hired man to start in bright and early."

"Oh, dear me! Oh, dear me!" cried Mrs. Bob-White. "Whatever shall we do? Our little ones can't fly well yet, and tomorrow the mower's sharp blade will surely catch them among the wheat!"

"Don't worry," said Bob-White. "For they will not cut the wheat tomorrow."

Nor did they cut the wheat when the next day came. The hired man fell down and stubbed his toe, and did not work at all that day.

That day the ten little Bob-Whites finished learning to fly. And by the time evening came they could lift themselves up into the air with a sudden whir, just like their parents, and could float away as easily and almost as far as Bob-White himself.

And Bob-White and Mrs. Bob-White were very happy, for now their little ones need not fear the sharp blade of the mower as it cut through the wheat.

"I saw the Farmer Man talking to his sons and his hired man at the edge of the wheat field today," said Bob-White.

"The Farmer Man is determined that the wheat shall be cut tomorrow, so he is going to cut it himself. And he says that all his sons and his hired man must help him, whether they feel well or not, so that the task may be finished quickly."

"Do you really think they will cut it this time?" asked Mrs. Bob-White.

"Yes, indeed!" said Bob-White. "A man may tell others to do his work, and the work may be done. But whenever a man himself starts doing his work, he is pretty sure to finish it."

"Well, let them cut it if they please," said Mrs. Bob-White. "Our little ones still have a few things to learn about the finer points of flying, before they can look after themselves. But already they can fly too well to be caught by the mower's sharp blade among the ripe wheat."

And sure enough, the next morning the Farmer Man and his sons and his hired man were up and in the wheat field bright and early.

And as they started reaping the wheat, the mowers' sharp blades cut through the tall stalks of wheat at a great rate.

As soon as they heard the mowers' sharp blades begin cutting the wheat, Bob-White and Mrs. Bob-White and all ten of the little Bob-Whites flew up into the air with a great whir of wings.

Then they all flew over to the next field, where they were perfectly safe from the mowers' sharp blades which were cutting so rapidly through the wheat.

And there Bob-White and his little mate taught the ten little Bob-Whites still more about flying, so that in a very short time all ten of them were always well able to take care of themselves.

BLUEBEARD

Once upon a time there lived a great lord who had many fine houses both in town and in the country. The dishes in his houses were of gold and silver. The furniture was covered with embroidery. The carriages and coaches shone with gold. But, sad to say, this man had a beard which was *blue!* This made him so terrifying that women and children fled in fright whenever he showed his face.

Now Bluebeard, for that was what everyone called him, had as a neighbor a lady of high degree with two handsome daughters. He proposed to her that she give him one of her daughters in marriage, leaving it to her to decide which one it should be. Neither of them wished to marry him, for who would want to be married to a man with a blue beard? Then, too, he had already had several wives, and no one knew what had become of them.

Bluebeard wanted very much to become well acquainted with these charming maidens, so he invited them with their mother and some other young people to one of his

country houses. Here they remained a whole week long, walking, hunting, and fishing. The rest of the time was spent at dances and banquets and delicious luncheons! Finally the younger sister began to think their host's beard not so blue after all, and that he was a very fine man! So, as soon as they returned to the city, their marriage took place.

A month passed. Then Bluebeard told his wife that he was obliged to go to the country for six weeks. He begged her to have the best of good times during his absence, and gave her permission to invite her dearest friends to visit her.

"Here," he said to her, "are the keys to the two great storerooms, and to the closet where the gold and silver dishes are kept. This is the key of my strong box, where you will find my gold and silver money, and the jewel caskets in which are all my precious stones. And this is the pass key to all the rooms in the house.

"And here is the little key which opens the door of the small room at the end of the great gallery below stairs. That little room you must not enter. Open everything, go everywhere, but into this one small room I forbid you even to look! If you do I shall be so angry there is no telling what I may do to you!"

Bluebeard's wife promised to do as he told her, so kissing her good-by, he stepped into his traveling coach and set out on his journey.

The young wife's neighbors and dearest friends at once hurried to call upon her, so anxious were they to inspect all the riches of her house. They dared not come while her husband was there, because he looked so fierce with his great blue beard! They examined all the closets and wardrobes, each of which was more crowded with beautiful things than the last.

They could not stop exclaiming over the good fortune of their friend, whom they had pitied before.

The young wife took no pleasure in this display of riches. Her mind was busy with just one thing—the forbidden door of the little room downstairs. So curious was she that she ran hastily down by a hidden stairway. When she reached the door, she stood still for a moment, thinking of what her husband had said to her. She trembled with fear, but her curiosity was so strong that she could not overcome it. She put the key in the lock, and opened wide the door of the forbidden room.

At first she could see nothing, for the shutters were all tightly closed. But as her eyes became accustomed to the dim light, she saw that the floor was covered with blood, and a number of dead bodies hung along the walls!

Here, then, were Bluebeard's other wives! He had cut off their heads, one after the other!

The poor girl almost died of fright. The key which she had taken from the lock slipped through her trembling fingers to the floor. Coming slowly to her senses, she picked it up, locked the door, and went upstairs. Then, to her horror, she noticed that the key of the secret chamber was flecked with blood. She wiped and wiped it, but the blood spot did not disappear. She washed it, and rubbed it with sand, but as

soon as the spot of blood was removed from one side, it appeared on the other, for it was a magic key.

Now that very afternoon Bluebeard returned from his journey, saying the business which had called him away had been settled in his favor. His wife did her best to make him think she was delighted at his unexpected return. The next morning he asked her for the keys. As she gave them back to him, her hands trembled so that he instantly guessed what had happened.

"How is it," he asked, "that the key of the little room downstairs is not here with the others?"

"I must have left it on my table," she said.

"Get it at once," said Bluebeard.

She returned without it, saying she had lost it. But at last, after several delays, she was obliged to bring it to her husband.

Bluebeard looked at it closely, and said to his wife, "Why is there blood upon this key?"

"I do not know," answered the poor lady, now paler than death.

"You do not know!" jeered Bluebeard. "You wanted to enter the secret room? Very well. Enter it and take your place among the ladies you found there."

The young wife threw herself at her husband's feet, weeping and begging for mercy. She was so lovely in her distress that she would have moved the heart of a stone, but Bluebeard's heart was much harder than any stone.

"You shall die at once!" he cried.

"If I must die," she begged, looking up at him through her tears, "give me time to say my prayers!"

"I will give you five minutes," said Bluebeard, turning away.

As soon as she was alone, she called her sister and said, "Dear Sister Anne, go up, I beg of you, to the very top of the tower and see if my brothers are in sight. They promised to visit me today. If you see them, signal them to hasten!"

So Sister Anne went up to the top of the high tower. She had scarcely reached the top when the poor lady cried softly, "Anne, Sister Anne, do you see anyone coming?"

And Sister Anne replied, "I see only the motes dancing in the sunbeams, and the grass growing green!"

Bluebeard, meanwhile, with his great cutlass, was waiting at the foot of the stairs for his wife.

"Come down here at once!" cried Bluebeard angrily, "or I shall come upstairs!"

"I am coming!" answered his wife. Again she cried very softly, "Anne, Sister Anne, do you see *nothing?*"

32

"I see," answered Sister Anne, "a great cloud of dust blowing across the road."

"Can it be my brothers?"

"Alas, no, my sister, I see only a flock of sheep."

"Are you coming down?" stormed Bluebeard.

"Just one minute more!" answered his wife. And for the last time she cried softly, "Anne, Sister Anne, do you see them coming?"

"I see," answered Sister Anne, "two horsemen riding this way, but they are still far off."

"God be praised!" she cried an instant later, "those are my brothers! I have made signs to them to hasten."

But Bluebeard now began to shout so loudly the whole house trembled and shook. The poor wife went down the stairs and threw herself at his feet, weeping and pleading.

"All that is of no use," said Bluebeard. "Die you must!"

With these words he twisted his left hand in her hair and swung the cutlass through the air to cut off her head. The poor woman turned her eyes up to him and begged for one moment to gather up her strength.

"No!" he thundered. "Commend yourself to God!"

At that very moment there was a loud knocking at the door. Bluebeard stopped short and dropped his arm. The door was thrown open, and in rushed the two brothers, who leaped straight at Bluebeard with their swords in their hands. He tried to escape, but they caught him just as he reached the doorstep. There they cut him in two with their swords and left him dead.

Bluebeard's widow became the mistress of his entire fortune. A part of it she expended in getting her sister happily wedded to a young gentleman of whom she had long been fond. Another portion was spent for a captain's commission for each of her beloved brothers. Then she married a good man, who made her forget the unhappy hours she had spent with Bluebeard.

TOM THUMB AND THE FAIRY TAILORS

TOM THUMB

Once upon a time, in the days of King Arthur, Merlin, the wizard, was making a long journey. He was an old man and grew weary, so he stopped at the cottage of an honest plowman to ask for food. The plowman's wife brought him milk and brown bread and set this homely fare before him as politely as if it had been cake and wine.

Merlin could not help seeing that the plowman and his wife looked sad, although their cottage was neat and they did not seem to be in want. He asked them the cause of their grief, and found it was that they had no children.

"Ah, me!" said the woman sadly, "if I but had a son, although he were no bigger than my husband's thumb, I should be the happiest woman in the world."

Now Merlin was much amused at the thought of a boy no bigger than a man's thumb, and as soon as he reached Fairyland he called on the queen of the fairies, who was a great friend of his. "On my journey," he said, "I had kind treatment from a plowman's wife who said she would be the happiest woman in the world if she could but have a son no bigger than her husband's thumb. Can you not grant her wish?"

"Indeed I can," laughed the fairy queen, "and I will."

And so it happened that the plowman's wife had a son who, to the wonder of the country folk, was no bigger than his father's thumb. But he was strong and healthy, so his size did not trouble his mother.

One summer morning wnen tne wee baby was only a few days old, the queen of the fairies flew in at the window of the room where he lay. She touched his cheek lightly with a butterfly kiss and gave him the name of Tom Thumb. She then ordered her fairy tailors to make for Tom a wonderful suit, his hat of an oak leaf, his shirt of a spider's web, his jacket of thistledown, his trousers of apple-rind, and his shoes of the skin of a mouse, nicely tanned, with the hair inside.

Tom never was bigger than his father's thumb, but as he grew older he became keen of wit and full of roguish tricks. Other boys

"Please, please," begged Tom, "let me out! let me out! I'll never do wrong again."

The boy soon let him out, and sure enough, Tom never tried to steal cherry stones again.

One day Tom's mother was beating up a batter pudding, and she put little Tom in an eggshell to keep him out of harm's way. While she had her back turned, Tom knocked a hole in the eggshell, crept out, and climbed to the edge of the bowl to see if his mother had stirred in any raisins. But his foot slipped and he fell head over heels into the batter.

His mother did not see him, and stirred him with the raisins into the pudding, which she then put into the pot to boil. Tom soon felt so warm that he began to kick and struggle, and his mother, seeing the pudding jump round and round in the pot in such a furious manner, thought it was bewitched. Just then a tramp came by, and she snatched the pudding out of the pot and gave it to him. He put it into his hat and trudged away, thinking how good that pudding would taste for supper.

did not like him very well because he was so sly, but sometimes they let him play at cherry stones with them. When he lost his cherry stones he used to creep into the other boys' bags, stuff a stone into each pocket, and come out again to play. One day as his head popped out of the mouth of a bag, its owner chanced to see him. "Ah, ha! my little Tom Thumb," cried the boy, "so I have caught you at your tricks at last! Now you shall pay for your thieving!"

Then the boy drew the string tight around Tom's neck and shook the bag so hard that the cherry stones bruised Tom's limbs and body quite as he deserved.

As soon as Tom could get the batter out of his mouth he began to shout, and this so frightened the tramp that he flung hat and pudding away and ran off as fast as he could. The pudding was broken into a dozen pieces by the fall and Tom, set free, went home to his mother. She wiped the dough from his face and his clothes, gave him one of the raisins for his supper, kissed him, and put him to bed.

Another time Tom Thumb's mother took him with her when she went to milk the cow. It was a very windy evening and she tied the little fellow with a needleful of thread to a thistle, that he might not be blown away. Tom had a fine time, swinging and singing and talking with the bees and butterflies. But by and by a big red cow came along and, taking a fancy to his oak-leaf hat, picked him and the thistle up at one mouthful. When the cow began to chew the thistle, Tom was dreadfully frightened at her great teeth, and called out: "Mother! Mother!"

"Where are you, my dear boy?"
cried his mother in alarm.
"Here, mother, here in the red
cow's mouth."

The mother began to weep and wring her hands, and Tom began to kick and bite and scratch so fiercely that the cow, thinking she had a bee in there tickling her mouth, was glad to let him drop out. His mother caught him up in her apron and ran home with him.

One day, as Tom Thumb was in the fields with his father, the boy begged to be allowed to take home the horse and cart. His father laughed at the thought of little Tom driving a horse, and asked him how he would hold the reins. "Oh," said Tom, "I will sit in the horse's ear, and call out which way he is to go." The father thought that was a fine notion, so he placed Tom in the horse's ear and off they started.

"Yeo hup! Yeo hup!" cried Tom, as he passed some country people on the road. The country people did not see Tom and thought the horse was bewitched, so they ran

off in a hurry. Tom's mother was much surprised to see the horse draw his cart up to the cottage door with no one to guide him, and ran out to learn what it meant. But Tom called to her: "Mother! Mother! Take me down; I am in the horse's ear!" Tom's mother was glad that her tiny son could be so useful. She lifted him gently down and gave him half a blackberry for his dinner.

After this, Tom's father made him a whip of barley straw, that he might sometimes drive the cow, and you may be sure Tom was very proud. As he was driving the cow home one day, he fell into one of her deep tracks and a raven picked up the straw, and Tom with it, and carried him to the top of a giant's castle by the seaside. There

he dropped him as not soft enough food for the baby ravens. Soon afterward Grumbo, the giant, came out to walk in his roof garden. He picked Tom Thumb up between his finger and thumb and looked him over to see if he was an ant or a beetle, and then opening his great mouth, tried to swallow him like a pill. But Tom so danced in the red throat of the giant that he was soon cast out into the sea.

Before Tom had a chance to be frightened, a big fish swallowed him down at a gulp. Not satisfied with Tom, the greedy fish also seized a fisherman's bait, and was whisked out upon the land. It was such a fine fish that it was sent as a present to King Arthur. When it was opened and Tom Thumb was found inside, everybody, especially Tom himself, was delighted.

The King made Tom the court dwarf, and he was soon a great favorite, for his tricks and gambols and lively speeches amused the Queen and the Knights of the Round Table. When the King went hunting he often took Tom with him. If it rained, Tom used to creep into the King's pocket and sleep until the rain was over.

One day King Arthur asked Tom about his parents. Tom told him they were poor country folk,

so the King led him into the royal treasury and told him to help himself to all the money he could carry, and take it home to his father and mother. Tom made a purse of a rat's ear and put into it a tiny silver coin not so large as a dime. With great difficulty he got it on his back and set out for his father's cottage half a mile away. After traveling two days and two nights, he reached home almost tired to death.

His mother let him in, and you may be sure both his parents were glad to see him. "Oh, mother!" he cried, "I have brought you enough money to make you rich. The King gave me all I could carry to bring home to you."

Then Tom opened his purse and out there rolled a threepenny bit.

One day Tom was taken sick. The queen of the fairies heard of his illness, and came in a chariot drawn by flying squirrels and took Tom back to Fairyland with her. There he soon grew strong and well again. After a while the fairy queen whistled for a wind that blew Tom Thumb back to the court. Just as he was whirling like a straw over the palace yard, the cook passed along with a great bowl of porridge, the King's favorite dish. Poor **Tom** fell splash into the royal porridge, which spattered up into the cook's eyes. The cook dropped the bowl, and the King's porridge was spilled.

"Oh, dear! Oh, dear!" cried Tom. And "Murder! Murder!" cried the cook.

The cook was a cross, red-faced old fellow, and swore to King Arthur that Tom had done it on purpose. So Tom was tried for high treason and sentenced to be beheaded. Just as this awful sentence was spoken, Tom saw a miller standing by, with his mouth wide open. He took a good spring and jumped down the miller's throat, and nobody thought of looking for him there.

The miller shut his mouth and went home, but he was not long at ease. Tom began to roll and tumble about, so that the miller thought himself bewitched and sent for a doctor. When the doctor came, Tom began to dance and sing. The doctor was more frightened than the miller, and he sent in a hurry for ten other doctors and twenty wise men. They all began to discuss the matter at great length, each insisting that his own explanation was the true one. The miller was so bored by all their wisdom that he couldn't help yawning, and while his mouth was open Tom seized the chance and jumped out on the table. The miller snatched him up in a fury and threw him out of the window into the millstream, where he was once more swallowed by a fish.

The fish was caught and sold in the market to a courteous knight, who sent it as a present to the queen. She gave orders that it be cooked for dinner. When the fish was opened, Tom once more popped out, and the cook ran with him to the King, who was so pleased to see Tom Thumb again that he forgave him for upsetting the porridge, ordered him a new suit of clothes, and made him, little as he was, a Knight of the Round Table. For a horse Tom had a scampering mouse, and for a sword he wore at his side a tailor's needle.

One bright day as Tom was riding with the King and his knights, a big black cat jumped down from a wall and caught both Tom and his steed. As the cat began to devour the poor mouse, Tom drew his sword and boldly charged the enemy. King Arthur and Lancelot, the bravest of the knights, rushed to his aid and rescued him just in time. The little hero was sadly scratched and his fine clothes were torn by the cat's claws. He was carried to the palace and laid on a bed of pigeon's down in a beautiful crystal salt-cellar to rest and get well. Then the queen of the fairies came and bore him away to Fairyland again, where she kept him years and years.

But Tom so teased to return to the court that one day the fairy queen dressed him in bright green and called a breeze to puff him back to earth. His coming was a great event. People flocked from far and near to look at the famous Tom Thumb, and he was carried in state to the palace.

But King Arthur, too, had gone away to Fairyland, and King Thunstone, the new King, did not know this little knight in green. He asked Tom who he was, where he came from, and where he lived, and Tom answered very politely, telling his whole story. The King was charmed with the wee man and his clever speech. He ordered a tiny chair to be made, so that Tom might sit on the King's table, and he had the royal architect build a palace of gold nine inches high, with a door an inch wide, for Tom Thumb to live in. The King also gave him a coach as big as an apple, drawn by six glossy mice.

Tom Thumb lived at the court of King Thunstone for many, many years, and did many wonderful deeds. And when he died the King and the whole court wore mourning for three days. They buried him under a rosebush with a wee white marble monument to mark his grave. If you should happen to come upon that rosebush, you would find his monument under it still.

BAD WOLF, "ARE THE APPLES NICE?"

THE THREE LITTLE PIGS

Once there was a Mother Pig who had Three Little Pigs. These Three Little Piggies ate the food their mother put before them, and went to bed early every night when their bedtime came, and in other ways did as they were told. So it was not very long until the Three Little Pigs had grown big and strong.

One day the eldest Little Pig said to his mother, "I am big and strong now, and soon will be really grownup. I must go out into the world to seek my fortune and build myself a little house to live in."

"Very well," said good old Mother Pig. "But beware of the Big Bad Wolf, my son, for he is very clever and his teeth are both long and sharp."

So the eldest Little Pig started out to make his way in the world and build himself a little house to live in.

After a while he came to a crossroads, and he took the road that led to the left through a big woods. On the other side of the woods the Little Pig met a man driving a cart loaded with nice clean straw.

"Oh, please, kind sir," said the Little Pig very politely, "you have such a great lot of straw, will you not give me some to make my house with?"

And the man, glad to have met such a well-mannered little pig, gave him all the straw he wanted.

Then the Little Pig set to work and worked hard, and soon he had built himself a fine house out of the straw.

It was not so very long after the house was finished that the Big Bad Wolf chanced to pass by, and he smelled the fat Little Pig inside.

"Well, well, well!" said the Wolf to himself. "Here's my dinner waiting for me!"

So he knocked on the door of the Little Pig's house, and called out in his sweetest voice, "Little Pig! Little Pig! A friend is here. Please open the door and let him in!"

But the Little Pig stuck his head out of an upper window and saw the Big Bad Wolf, and then he remembered what his mother had told him.

"No! No! No! by the hair of my
  chinny-chin-chin!
Your teeth are long and sharp; I
  will not let you in!"

cried the Little Pig. "You are no friend, but the Big Bad Wolf!"

This made the Big Bad Wolf very, very angry, so he showed his long sharp teeth and roared:

"Little Pig! Little Pig! Let me in!
  Let me in!
Or I'll huff and I'll puff and I'll
  blow your house down!"

But the Little Pig did not dare let him in.

So the Big Bad Wolf huffed and he puffed, and pretty soon—sure

enough—he blew down the Little Pig's house. But the Little Pig had slipped away into the woods, so the Big Bad Wolf didn't make a dinner of him after all.

It was not very long before the second Little Pig began to long to see the world.

"I must go out into the world to seek my fortune," he said one day, "and build myself a little house to live in."

"Very well," said good old Mother Pig. "But beware of the Big Bad Wolf, my son, for he is very clever and his teeth are both long and sharp."

"PLEASE, KIND SIR, GIVE ME SOME WOOD"

So the second Little Pig started out to make his way in the world and build himself a little house to live in.

When he came to the crossroads he took the road to the right. Before long, just on the other side of a thicket, he met a man with a cart full of wood.

"Oh, please, kind sir," said the second Little Pig, very politely, "you have such a great lot of wood, will you not give me some to make my house with?"

And the man, glad to have met such a well-mannered little pig, gave him all the wood he wanted. Then the second Little Pig set to work and worked hard, and soon he had built himself a fine house out of the wood.

It was not so very long after the house was finished that the Big Bad Wolf chanced to pass by that way and he smelled the fat Little Pig inside the house.

"Well, well, well!" said the Wolf to himself. "Here's my dinner waiting for me!"

So he knocked on the door of the second Little Pig's house, and called out in his sweetest voice, "Little Pig! Little Pig! A friend is here. Open the door and let him in!"

But the second Little Pig saw the Big Bad Wolf's paws through

LITTLE PIGGY BUILDING HIS HOUSE OF WOOD

the keyhole, and he remembered what his mother had told him.

"No! No! No! by the hair of my chinny-chin-chin!
Your teeth are long and sharp; I will not let you in!"

cried the second Little Pig. "You're no friend, but the Big Bad Wolf!"

This made the Big Bad Wolf very angry indeed, so he showed his long sharp teeth and roared:

"Little Pig! Little Pig! Let me in! Let me in!
Or I'll huff and I'll puff and I'll blow your house down!"

But the second Little Pig did not dare let him in.

45

THE SECOND LITTLE PIG HID IN THE THICKET

So the Big Bad Wolf huffed and he puffed, and pretty soon—sure enough—he blew down the second Little Pig's house. But the second Little Pig had slipped out the back door and hidden in the thicket, so the Big Bad Wolf didn't make a dinner of him after all.

Before very long the last Little Pig grew tired of staying at home.

"I must go out into the world and seek my fortune," said he one day, "and build myself a little house to live in."

"Very well," said good old Mother Pig, sorry to have him go, for now she would be all alone.

"But beware of the Big Bad Wolf, my son, for his teeth are long and sharp."

So the last Little Pig set out to make his way in the world and build himself a house to live in.

When he came to the crossroads the third Little Pig did not turn aside as his brothers had done, but followed the road straight ahead. And by and by he met a man with a big wagon full of bricks and lime.

"Oh, please, kind sir," said the last Little Pig, very politely, "you have such a great lot of bricks and lime, will you not give me some to build my house with?"

And the man, glad to have met such a well-mannered little pig, gave him some bricks and lime.

Then the last Little Piggy set to work and worked very hard, mixing mortar and laying the bricks, so that it was not long until he had built himself a fine little house.

And once again it happened that the Big Bad Wolf chanced to pass by shortly after the house was finished, and he smelled the fat Little Pig inside.

"Well, well, well!" said the Wolf to himself. "Here's my dinner waiting for me, and it shall not get away from me this time!"

THE BIG BAD WOLF HUFFED AND PUFFED, BUT THE STRONG LITTLE HOUSE WOULD NOT BLOW DOWN

So he knocked on the door of the last Little Pig's fine new house, and called out in his sweetest voice, "Little Pig! Little Pig! A friend has come to call. Open the door and let him in!"

But the last Little Pig peeped through the keyhole, and saw the Big Bad Wolf's glittering eyes. And they made Little Piggy think of what his mother had told him, and he cried out:

"No! No! No! by the hair of my chinny-chin-chin!
Your teeth are long and sharp; I will not let you in!"

"You are no friend at all," the Little Pig went on. "You are the Big Bad Wolf, and you want to eat me up!"

This made the Big Bad Wolf very angry indeed, so he showed his long white teeth and snarled:

"Little Pig! Little Pig! Let me in! Let me in!
Or I'll huff and I'll puff and I'll blow your house down!"

The last Little Pig would not let him in, however, but just laughed and said, "You may huff and you may puff, but you'll never get me!"

So the Big Bad Wolf drew in a big, big breath, and then he huffed

47

THE LITTLE PIGGY INSIDE LAUGHED

and he puffed until he grew red in the face. But the strong little house would not blow down, and the Little Piggy inside just laughed.

This made the Big Bad Wolf angrier than ever, and he huffed and he puffed and he puffed and he huffed his very hardest, until he grew blue in the face, but he couldn't even shake the little brick house.

At last he huffed and he puffed so much that he could huff and puff no more, and he knew he could never blow that house down. He lay down on the ground to rest and to think of a better way to get the Little Piggy for his dinner.

"Little Pig! Little Pig!" he called at last, when he had caught his breath again. "I know where there is a fine field of turnips."

"Do you?" said the Little Piggy. "And where is that?"

"I'll show you," said the Wolf. "Just be ready early in the morning, and I'll come by for you at six o'clock. Then we can go together down to Farmer Jones's field and get the turnips."

"I'll be ready," promised the Little Pig, and he laughed to himself as the Big Bad Wolf trotted away.

In the morning the last Little Pig got up very early, and at five o'clock he was out in the turnip field rooting up turnips and filling his basket with them. Then he hurried home again, and had a nice potful of turnips cooking on the fire when six o'clock came and the Big Bad Wolf knocked on his door.

"Little Pig! Little Pig! Aren't you ready?" called the Wolf. "It's six o'clock, and time to start after the turnips."

"Oh, I'm so sorry!" said the Little Pig. "I was afraid you weren't coming, so I went ahead at five o'clock. I've been to the field and back again, with all the turnips I can eat."

Then the Big Bad Wolf grew red with rage, but he didn't let on, thinking that he could fool Little

Piggy some other way, and so get him for his dinner. So he just pretended to laugh, and said, "Turnips are all very well, but I know of something far better."

"What is that?" asked the Little Pig.

"Apples—such fine, sweet, juicy apples," said the Wolf. "There's a big tree full of them down back of Farmer Brown's barn. If you'll come with me at five o'clock in the morning, we'll get all we can carry home."

"Splendid!" said Piggy, laughing to himself. "Just come by for me at five o'clock sharp, and we'll go for them." And he laughed again as the Wolf trotted away.

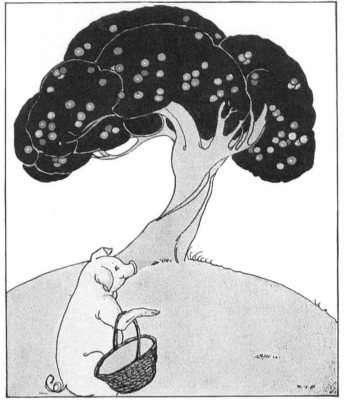

LITTLE PIGGY ON HIS WAY FOR APPLES

Now Little Piggy thought he would fool the Big Bad Wolf again, so at four o'clock the next morning he took his basket and went down to the apple tree.

But the Big Bad Wolf had been fooled once, and he wasn't so easily fooled a second time, so he, too, set out for the apple tree long before five o'clock.

The Little Pig had climbed up into the apple tree and had just finished filling his basket with fine ripe apples.

Then he started to climb down to the ground. And just as he started to climb down the tree, whom should he see just below him but the Big Bad Wolf, grinning

AT FIVE O'CLOCK THE LITTLE PIG WAS OUT
ROOTING UP TURNIPS

49

LITTLE PIGGY FILLED HIS BASKET WITH APPLES

hungrily up at him and showing all of his sharp white teeth! My, my! but wasn't Little Piggy surprised and frightened!

"Good morning," said the Wolf. "What an early bird you are! Are the apples nice?"

"The best I've ever tasted," answered the Little Pig. "Here, I'll toss one down to you."

The Wolf made ready to catch it, but the Little Pig threw it so far that the Big Bad Wolf had to run for it, and then chase it along the ground as it rolled and bounced. And while he was trying to get it, the Little Pig jumped down

from the tree and ran home as fast as he could run. And then wasn't the Big Bad Wolf angry when he found that Little Piggy had fooled him again!

But the next day he made up his mind to try again. So he went to the Little Pig's house, and in his sweetest voice called out, "Little Pig! Little Pig! You are so clever that I want to be friends with you. And to show you how much I like you, I want to take you to the fair at the village this afternoon."

"Thank you," said the Little Pig. "I'll be glad to go. What time shall we start?"

"At three o'clock sharp," said the Big Bad Wolf, "so be sure and be ready."

Then he trotted off, sure that he would get Piggy this time.

But the Little Pig did not wait until three o'clock—no, indeed! He started just as soon as the Big Bad Wolf was out of sight, and he had a wonderful time at the fair. He rode on the merry-go-round until he was dizzy, and drank lemonade, and ate popcorn and ice-cream cones until he wasn't hungry at all any more. Then he looked around for something to buy and take home, to remind him of the good time he had had.

At last he bought a big, round butter churn and started off for home with it as fast as he could go. You see, it was now getting near three o'clock, and he wanted to be safe in his strong little brick house before the Big Bad Wolf came by for him.

The big churn was hard to carry, though, and he wasn't able to go very fast. So much time did the Little Pig lose that at last, just as he reached the top of the last big hill at the foot of which stood his little house, he caught sight of the Big Bad Wolf.

The Big Bad Wolf had just turned away from the door of the empty little brick house, and was starting up the hill.

Little Piggy trembled with terror, and looked about for a place to hide. Not a hiding place could he find—except the big churn he was carrying!

So the Little Pig crawled into the big butter churn to hide, as quick as he could, and started to pull the lid down over him. As he tugged at the lid, he shook the big, round churn about, and it started rolling down the hill—bumpety-bumpety, bumpety-bump!

The Big Bad Wolf heard the strange sound, and looked up the hill.

INTO THE CHURN CRAWLED LITTLE PIGGY

There he saw some strange, rolling thing rushing down upon him, making queer bumpety-bumpety noises that were very startling. He watched it come nearer, and then—frightened by the strange thing that did not seem in the least afraid of him—he turned tail and ran away as fast as he could to hide in his den.

The Little Pig in the churn rolled right up to his own doorstep, and there he thankfully carried his butter churn inside.

A little while later the Big Bad Wolf came back again. "Little Pig! Little Pig!" he called. "Are you going to the fair?"

51

"Oh," said the Little Pig, "I have been to the fair, and have come home again."

"And did you see a queer rolling thing as you came home, a dreadful thing that made queer noises as it rolled?" asked the Big Bad Wolf. "I had started for the fair when I met it, and it chased me for miles and miles!"

"Ha, ha!" laughed Piggy. "That was I, bringing home my new butter churn. Did I frighten you very badly?"

But the Big Bad Wolf just roared and roared with rage. He jumped up on the roof of the little brick house, and started to climb down the chimney after the Little Pig inside. He was so angry at being fooled again that nothing would satisfy him except eating Little Piggy for dinner.

The Little Pig heard The Big Bad Wolf in the chimney, and quickly kindled up the little fire on the hearth until it was blazing high. And then, when the Big Bad Wolf got near the bottom of the chimney he dropped — kerflump — right into the roaring hot fire!

What a howl the Wolf made! He burned his tail, and he scorched his back, and he singed his whiskers, and he got smoke in his eyes and ashes in his nose! And then he climbed right back up the chimney just as fast as he could climb!

Once outside again, he fled far away, howling as he ran, with the pain of his burns.

So far away did the Big Bad Wolf go that he was never heard of again, but Little Piggy lived happily forever after in his fine little brick house.

THE GOOSE GIRL

Once there was a beautiful Princess, the daughter of an old, widowed queen. This Princess was betrothed to a Prince who lived far away, and as the time for the marriage drew near she made ready to set forth on her journey to his country. Now the old queen loved her daughter very, very dearly and packed for her many rare and costly things—jewels and laces and fine dresses—everything that became a royal bride. And she gave her a waiting-maid to ride with her, and each had a horse for the journey. The Princess's horse was white and the maid's was sorrel. The white horse was called Falada, and it could speak.

When the time came for the Princess to go, the mother cut off a lock of her own white hair and gave it to her daughter, saying: "Take care of this, dear child; it is a charm that may help you."

The mother and daughter took sorrowful leave of each other, and the Princess set off on her journey.

As the Princess and her maid were riding along by a clear, tinkling brook, the Princess felt very thirsty and said gently: "Please get down and fetch me some water in my golden cup."

"Nay," said the maid, "if you are thirsty, get down and lie by the water and drink like a dog. I shall not be your waiting-maid any longer."

The Princess was so thirsty she dismounted and knelt over the little brook and drank from her hands, for the maid had her golden cup and she dared not ask for it. Her tears fell into the water as she sighed: "Alas! what will become of me?"

Then the lock of her mother's hair that she wore in her bosom answered her and said:

"Alas! Could thy mother know thy state,
Sadly would she bewail thy fate!"

With not a word of rebuke to the maid for her unkindness, the Princess mounted Falada again. They rode on and the day grew so warm that once more the Princess began to feel very thirsty. In her thoughts of her mother and of the Prince she had forgotten her maid's rude speech, and when they came to a sparkling stream, she said again: "Please get down and fetch me some water in my golden cup."

But the maid answered her even more insolently than before: "Drink up the whole river if you will, but I shall not fetch you water. I am no longer your waiting-maid."

The Princess was so thirsty she dismounted and lay down with her face upon the water and drank from the running stream. Again her tears fell into the ripples and she cried softly: "What will become of me?"

"Alas! Could thy mother know thy state,
Sadly would she bewail thy fate!"

So answered the lock of hair in her bosom, but as she leaned so low to drink, the lock fell into the stream and floated away. The Princess did not see it, but her wicked maid saw it and was glad, for she knew the hair had a magic spell, and saw that the poor bride would be in her power now that the charm was lost. So when the Princess would have sprung upon Falada again, the maid said sharply: "I shall ride upon Falada, and you may have my horse instead. And I shall wear your royal raiment, and you may have these common garments of mine."

The gentle Princess was afraid and gave her beautiful clothes to the cruel waiting-maid, while she herself put on the maid's plain dress. Then she climbed upon the sorrel horse and sadly watched the girl mount her white Falada.

As they drew near the city where the Prince lived, the false-hearted servant drew a sharp knife from her

so young and homesick it troubled him, and a great king must not be troubled; so he went to the door of the splendid chamber and called to the bride: "Who is the girl that came with you and is waiting in the court below?"

"I brought her with me for sake of company on the road," called back the maid. "Please your majesty, give her some work to do, that she may not be idle. She is good only for coarse and common work."

For some time the King could not think of any work for one who looked so childish and so delicate, but at last he said: "I have a lad who takes care of my geese; she may help him." Now the name of the lad was Conrad.

girdle and said: "I will kill you if you do not promise never, never to tell any one what has happened." And the poor little Princess, feeling in her bosom for the lock of her mother's hair and finding it gone, promised. But Falada saw it all and marked it well. At last they came to the royal court and great was the joy at their coming. The Prince ran to meet them and lifted the maid from Falada, thinking she was the one who was to be his wife, for he had never seen the Princess. The wicked servant was led to a splendid chamber, but the true princess stood unheeded in the court below.

Soon the old king happened to look out of a window and saw the girl in her common clothes. She looked

Soon afterward the false bride said to the Prince: "Dear my lord, will you do me a favor?"

"That I will," replied the Prince.

"Tell one of your servants," she said, "to cut off the head of the white horse I rode upon, for it was very unruly and plagued me sadly on the road." This she asked because she feared Falada would tell how she had treated the Princess. The Prince did as she wished, and the faithful Falada was killed.

Now when the true Princess heard of it she wept, and begged the servant to fasten up the head against the great gate of the city through which she had to pass every morning and evening. "Then," she said, "I can still see Falada."

It was hard to refuse so gentle a pleader anything, so the servant nailed the horse's head above the dark gate.

Early the next morning, as the true princess and Conrad went through the gate, she said sorrowfully:

"Falada, Falada, that thou shouldst
  hang there!"

And the head answered:

"Princess, that thou such wrong
  shouldst bear!
Alas! Could thy mother know thy
  state,
Sadly would she bewail thy fate!"

Then they went on driving the geese before them. When they came

to the meadow, the Princess seated herself on a bank of violets and let down her waving locks. Her hair was all of purest gold, and when Conrad saw it glitter in the sun, he ran up and would have pulled out a handful, but she cried:

"O wind, blow Conrad's hat away!
  May he chase it far over hill and lea,
  While I my golden locks array,
  The only crown that's left to me."

At once there came a puff of wind that snatched off Conrad's hat. Away it flew and he after it, and by the time he came back, the Princess had combed and curled her hair and put it up again. Conrad was angry and sulky and would not speak to her, but she helped him watch the geese until evening and then drive them homeward.

The next morning, as they were going through the dark gate, the

poor girl looked up at Falada's head and cried:

"Falada, Falada, that thou shouldst hang there!"

And it answered:

"Princess, that thou such wrong shouldst bear!
Alas! Could thy mother know thy state,
Sadly would she bewail thy fate!"

Again, when they reached the meadow, she began to comb her hair, and again Conrad ran and tried to take hold of it. But she cried quickly:

"O wind, blow Conrad's hat away!
May he chase it far over hill and lea,
While I my golden locks array,
The only crown that's left to me."

And again the wind came and blew his hat far away, so that he had to run after it; and when he came back the Princess had done up her hair and all was safe.

When they reached home that evening, Conrad went in a rage to the old King and said: "I will not have that girl to keep the geese with me any longer."

"Why not?" asked the King.

"Because she does nothing all day long but tease me," pouted Conrad.

"Tell me all that has happened," demanded the King.

Conrad replied: "Every morning when we go through the dark gate with our geese, she weeps, and talks with the white horse's head that hangs upon the wall. She says:

'Falada, Falada, that thou shouldst hang there!'

And the head answers:

'Princess, that thou such wrong shouldst bear!
Alas! Could thy mother know thy state,
Sadly would she bewail thy fate!'"

And Conrad went on telling what had happened in the meadow where the geese fed; how his hat was blown away, and he was forced to run after it and leave his flock, but he said nothing about his attempts to pull out some of the goose girl's hair. Then the old king told him to go out with her one day more and to tie on his hat with a string.

When morning came the King hid behind the dark gate and heard the goose girl speak to Falada and heard Falada answer. Then he went into the field and hid himself in a bush by the meadow's side. And by and by here came Conrad and the goose girl driving the flock. After a little while the King saw her let down her hair that glittered in the sun. He saw Conrad snatch at it and heard her say:

"O wind, blow Conrad's hat away!
  May he chase it far over hill and lea,
  While I my golden locks array,
  The only crown that's left to me."

Then there came a sudden breeze that carried away Conrad's hat, string and all, while the girl went on combing and curling her hair. All this the old King saw and went home without having been seen himself. When the goose girl came back in the evening, he summoned her to the throne room and asked her why she did all these strange things.

"Alas! Alas!" she cried, "I may not tell you, nor any man, or I shall lose my life." The kind old king urged her and urged her, but she only shook her golden head.

Finally he rose and went away, calling back over his shoulder: "If thou wilt not tell thy sorrows to a king, tell them to the stove."

The poor girl took him at his word, crept into the cold empty oven of the huge stove, and began to weep and relate all her sad story.

She was so unhappy it helped her to talk even to the stove, though it had a heart of iron. "Alas!" she cried, "here am I deserted by the whole world and forced to tend stupid geese, and yet I am a king's daughter. And to think that my false waiting-maid should now be wearing my bridal raiment and living in the prince's palace, while I am one of the meanest of his servants! If the queen, my mother, did but know it, her heart would break."

Now the old King was listening by the stovepipe and heard all the poor Princess said. At once he bade her come out of the oven, and had the ladies-in-waiting dress her in royal garments. Everybody at the court was astonished to see how beautiful she was. And you may be sure that when the Prince caught sight of her, he sent the wicked serving-maid away in her own old clothes and married the true princess, whom he loved so well that they lived happy ever after.

HENNY PENNY

One day Henny Penny wandered into the woods to search for nuts that had fallen to the ground. And as she was going along what should happen but—bingo!—a big acorn fell from a tree above her and hit her upon her poor bald head.

"Cut-cut-cut-cut!" squawked poor Henny Penny. "Oh, goodness! Oh, gracious! The sky's a-falling, surely! I must go and tell the King!"

And straightway Henny Penny set out to find the King and tell him that the sky was beginning to fall, for she thought he ought to know about it.

So she hurried along, and hurried along, and in a little while she met Cocky Locky.

"Cock-a-doodle-doo!" called Cocky Locky. "Good morning to you, Henny Penny, and where are you going this fine day?"

"Oh, deary me, Cocky Locky!" cried Henny Penny. "It isn't a good morning and it isn't a fine day! I went into the woods to gather nuts, and a piece of the sky fell on my poor bald head, so I'm on my way to tell the King the sky's a-falling."

"Oh, what a dreadful thing! Cock-a-doodle-doo!" exclaimed Cocky Locky. "Do you mind if I come along with you?"

"Not at all," said Henny Penny. "We'll both go and tell the King."

So they hurried along, and hurried along, Henny Penny and Cocky Locky, and as they hurried along, whom should they meet but Ducky Lucky.

"Quack! quack! quack!" called Ducky Lucky. "Good morning to you, Henny Penny and Cocky Locky, and where are the two of you going this fine day?"

"Oh, deary me, Ducky Lucky!" cried Cocky Locky. "It isn't a good morning and it isn't a fine day! Henny Penny went into the woods to gather nuts, and a piece of the sky fell upon her poor bald head, so we're on our way to tell the King the sky's a-falling."

"Oh, what a dreadful thing! Quack! quack!" exclaimed Ducky Lucky. "Do you mind if I come along with you?"

"Not at all," said Cocky Locky. "All three of us will go and tell the King."

HENNY PENNY AND COCKY LOCKY AND DUCKY LUCKY ON THEIR WAY TO THE KING

So they all hurried along, and hurried along, Henny Penny and Cocky Locky and Ducky Lucky, and as they hurried along, whom should they meet but Drakey Lakey.

"Quock! quock! quock!" called Drakey Lakey, for he was a little hoarse, as usual, and couldn't give a real quack. "Good morning to you, Henny Penny and Cocky Locky and Ducky Lucky, and where are the three of you going this fine day?"

"Oh, deary me, Drakey Lakey!" cried Ducky Lucky. "It isn't a good morning and it isn't a fine day! Henny Penny went into the woods to gather nuts, and a piece of the sky fell upon her poor bald head, so we're on our way to tell the King the sky's a-falling."

"Oh, what a dreadful thing! Quock! quock!" exclaimed Drakey Lakey. "Do you mind if I come along with you?"

"Not at all," said Ducky Lucky. "All four of us will tell the King."

So they all hurried along, and hurried along, Henny Penny and Cocky Locky and Ducky Lucky and

60

"HONK! HONK!" CALLED GOOSEY LOOSEY

Drakey Lakey, and as they hurried along, whom should they meet but Goosey Loosey.

"Honk! honk! honk!" called out Goosey Loosey. "Good morning to you, Henny Penny and Cocky Locky and Ducky Lucky and Drakey Lakey, and where are the four of you going this fine day?"

"Oh, deary me, Goosey Loosey!" cried Drakey Lakey. "It isn't a good morning and it isn't a fine day! Henny Penny went into the woods to gather nuts, and a piece of the sky fell upon her poor bald head, so we're on our way to tell the King the sky's a-falling."

"Oh, what a dreadful thing! Honk! honk!" exclaimed Goosey Loosey. "Do you mind if I come along with you?"

"Not at all," said Drakey Lakey. "All five of us will go and tell the King."

So they hurried along, and hurried along, Henny Penny and Cocky Locky and Ducky Lucky and Drakey Lakey and Goosey Loosey, and as they hurried along, whom should they meet but Gander Lander.

"Squonk! squonk! squonk!" called Gander Lander. "Good morning to you, Henny Penny and Cocky Locky and Ducky Lucky and Drakey Lakey and Goosey Loosey, and where are the five of you going this fine day?"

"Oh, deary me, Gander Lander!" cried Goosey Loosey. "It isn't a good morning and it isn't a fine day! Henny Penny went into the woods to gather nuts, and a piece of the sky fell upon her poor bald head, so we're on our way to tell the King the sky's a-falling."

"Oh, what a dreadful thing! Squonk! squonk!" exclaimed Gander Lander. "Do you mind if I come along with you?"

"Not at all," said Goosey Loosey. "All six of us will go and tell the King."

"OH, DEARY ME!" CRIED GANDER LANDER

So they all hurried along, and hurried along, Henny Penny and Cocky Locky and Ducky Lucky and Drakey Lakey and Goosey Loosey and Gander Lander, and as they hurried along, whom should they meet but Turkey Lurkey.

"Gobble! gobble! gobble!" called Turkey Lurkey, stretching out his long neck. "Good morning to you, Henny Penny and Cocky Locky and Ducky Lucky and Drakey Lakey and Goosey Loosey and Gander Lander, and where are the six of you going this fine day?"

"Oh, deary me, Turkey Lurkey!" cried Gander Lander. "It isn't a good morning and it isn't a fine day! Henny Penny went into the woods to gather nuts, and a piece of the sky fell upon her poor bald head, so we're on our way to tell the King the sky's a-falling."

"Oh, what a dreadful thing! Gobble! gobble!" exclaimed Turkey Lurkey. Do you mind if I come along with you?"

"Not at all," said Gander Lander. "All seven of us will go and tell the King."

So they all hurried along, and hurried along, Henny Penny and Cocky Locky and Ducky Lucky and Drakey Lakey and Goosey Loosey and Gander Lander and

A BIG ACORN HIT HENNY PENNY
UPON HER POOR BALD HEAD

Turkey Lurkey, all bound to tell the King the sky was falling.

And as they all hurried along, whom should they meet but Foxy Loxy!

"Good morning to you, my pretty friends," called Foxy Loxy, smiling slyly upon them all.

"And where are the seven of you going in such a hurry this fine day?"

"Oh, deary me, Foxy Loxy!" cried Turkey Lurkey. "It isn't a good morning and it isn't a fine day! Henny Penny went into the woods to gather nuts, and a piece

"GOOD MORNING, MY PRETTY FRIENDS,"
SAID FOXY LOXY

of the sky fell upon her poor bald head, so we're on our way to tell the King the sky's a-falling."

"Oh, what a dreadful thing!" exclaimed Foxy Loxy, but he smiled as though he thought it might not be such a dreadful thing, after all.

"And was Henny Penny standing near the big oak tree at the edge of the woods, may I ask?"

"That was just the place!" cried Henny Penny.

"Ah, I thought so," said Foxy Loxy, smiling more broadly than ever. "I was there yesterday, and I thought the sky looked rather weak there. The King should know' about it, by all means, but are you sure that you know the way to the King's palace?"

Turkey Lurkey looked at Gander Lander, Gander Lander looked at Goosey Loosey, Goosey Loosey looked at Drakey Lakey, Drakey Lakey looked at Ducky Lucky, Ducky Lucky looked at Cocky Locky, Cocky Locky looked at Henny Penny, and Henny Penny shook her head.

"Then I shall lead you to it," said Foxy Loxy, and he licked his lips hungrily. "I know the King well, and I can find his palace for you very easily. Just follow me, and we'll all go and tell the King the sky's a-falling."

So Foxy Loxy led the way, and behind him followed Turkey Lurkey and Gander Lander and Goosey Loosey and Drakey Lakey and Ducky Lucky and Cocky Locky and Henny Penny, all going to tell the King that the sky was falling.

They hurried along, and hurried along, and presently they came to a big hole that went deep into a bank beneath the roots of a tree.

Now this was really the door to Foxy Loxy's den, but Foxy Loxy smiled and said: "This is a short way to the King's palace. I shall go in first, and you must follow me, one at a time. Then, very soon, you will all be in the presence of the King, to tell him the sky's a-falling."

Henny Penny and all her companions were very grateful to Foxy Loxy for showing them the way to the King's palace, and they promised to do just as he said. So Foxy Loxy smiled slyly, and went on into his burrow.

There he waited, just around a turn at the far end, and as he waited for them to come to him he thought of what a fine dinner Henny Penny and her friends would make for him.

Henny Penny started toward the big hole in the bank. Then, all at once, she remembered something.

ALL AT ONCE HENNY PENNY REMEMBERED SOMETHING

"Oh goodness gracious me!" she cried, stopping short. "I have forgotten to lay my egg today! There are enough of you to go and tell the King without me. I must be off at once!" and away went Henny Penny as fast as she could go, straight toward her box in the barnyard.

Cocky Locky started toward the big hole. Just then, all at once, he remembered something.

"Dear! dear!" he exclaimed, shaking his red comb. "Just think, there has been no crowing done in the barnyard for hours! There are enough of you to tell the King without me, so I shall get back to my work." And away he hurried also.

Ducky Lucky and Drakey Lakey and Goosey Loosey and Gander Lander and Turkey Lurkey looked after him.

And as they looked after him, they all began to think of things they should be doing instead of going to see the King.

"Foxy Loxy knows the King, and the way to his palace," said Goosey Loosey. "Let him tell the King the sky's a-falling. I have my work to do, and I must get back to it at once."

"So must we," said all the others, and so away they hurried, leaving Foxy Loxy himself to go and tell the King that the sky was falling.

Foxy Loxy, back in his dark den, waited hungrily for Henny Penny and her friends to come to him, and after he had waited a long, long time he began to wonder what could have happened to them. So he left his den and went out to the mouth of his burrow to look for them.

And then wasn't he a surprised and angry Foxy Loxy!

He found them gone, every one of them—Henny Penny and Cocky Locky and Ducky Lucky and Drakey Lakey and Goosey Loosey and Gander Lander and Turkey Lurkey!

And thus it was that sly Foxy Loxy had to go without his fine dinner, and the King was never told that the sky was falling.

WHEN THE LITTLE SMALL WEE BEAR LOOKED AT HIS BED, THERE LAY GOLDILOCKS, FAST ASLEEP

THE THREE BEARS

Once upon a time there were Three Bears who lived together in a little house of their own in the woods.

One of them was a Little Small Wee Bear, one was a Middle-sized Bear, and the other was a Great Big Bear.

They each had a bowl for their porridge. The Little Small Wee Bear had a little bowl, the Middle-sized Bear had a middle-sized bowl, and the Great Big Bear had a great big bowl.

And they each had a chair to sit in. The Little Small Wee Bear had a little wee chair, the Middle-sized Bear had a middle-sized chair, and the Great Big Bear had a great big chair.

And also they each had a bed to sleep in. The Little Small Wee Bear had a tiny little bed, the Middle-sized Bear had a middle-sized bed, and the Great Big Bear had a great huge bed.

One morning after they had made the porridge for their breakfast and poured it into their porridge bowls, the Three Bears went for a walk in the wood while their porridge cooled, for they did not want to burn their mouths by trying to eat it too soon.

While they were walking in the wood, a little girl, whose name was Goldilocks, came to the house.

She could not have been a good, well-brought-up little girl, for first she looked in at the window, and then she peeped in at the keyhole, and seeing nobody in the house, she lifted the latch.

The door was not fastened at all, because the Bears were good Bears, who did nobody any harm and never suspected that anybody would harm them.

So Goldilocks opened the door and went in, and she was well pleased when she saw the porridge on the table.

If she had been a good little girl, she would have waited until the Bears came home, for they were good Bears—a little rough perhaps, as the manner of Bears is—but for all that, very good-natured and hospitable.

But Goldilocks was a naughty little girl, and she set about helping herself.

GOLDILOCKS EATING THE LITTLEST BEAR'S PORRIDGE

First she tasted the porridge of the Great Big Bear, and that was too hot for her. And then she tasted the porridge of the Middle-sized Bear, but that was too cold for her. And then she went to the porridge of the Little Small Wee Bear, and tasted that.

And that was neither too hot nor too cold, but just right, and she liked it so well that she ate it all up.

When she was no longer hungry, Goldilocks went into the parlor to see what she could find, and there she saw the three chairs.

First she tried sitting in the chair of the Great Big Bear, but

that was too hard for her. And then she sat down in the chair of the Middle-sized Bear, but that was too soft for her. And last of all she sat down in the chair of the Little Small Wee Bear, and that was neither too hard nor too soft, but just right.

So she seated herself in it, and there she sat and sat until the bottom of the chair came out, and down she came, plump, upon the floor!

Then Goldilocks went upstairs into the bedchamber in which the Three Bears slept.

And first she lay down upon the bed of the Great Big Bear, but that

THE BOTTOM OF THE CHAIR CAME OUT
AND DOWN CAME GOLDILOCKS!

was too high at the head for her. And next she lay down upon the bed of the Middle-sized Bear, and that was too high at the foot for her. And then she lay down upon the bed of the Little Small Wee Bear, and that was neither too high at the head nor too high at the foot, but just right.

So she covered herself up comfortably and lay there until she fell fast asleep.

By this time the Three Bears thought their porridge would be cool enough, so they came home to breakfast.

Now Goldilocks had left the spoon of the Great Big Bear standing in his porridge, and he noticed it, first thing.

"SOMEBODY HAS BEEN AT MY PORRIDGE!"

said the Great Big Bear, in his great, rough, gruff voice.

And when the Middle-sized Bear looked at his porridge, he saw that the spoon was standing in his porridge, too.

"SOMEBODY HAS BEEN AT MY PORRIDGE!"

said the Middle-sized Bear, in his middle-sized voice.

Then the Little Small Wee Bear looked at his porridge, and there was the spoon in his bowl also, but the porridge was all gone.

"SOMEBODY HAS BEEN AT MY PORRIDGE, AND HAS EATEN IT ALL UP!"

cried the Little Small Wee Bear, in his little, small, wee voice.

Upon this the Three Bears, seeing that some one had entered their house and eaten up the Little Small Wee Bear's breakfast, began to look about.

Now Goldilocks had not put the hard cushion straight when she rose from the chair of the Great Big Bear, and when he came into the parlor he noticed it, first thing.

"SOMEBODY HAS BEEN SITTING IN MY CHAIR!"

said the Great Big Bear, in his great, rough, gruff voice.

"SOMEBODY HAS BEEN SITTING IN MY CHAIR!"
SAID THE MIDDLE-SIZED BEAR

WHEN GOLDILOCKS SAW THE THREE BEARS, UP SHE STARTED, TUMBLED OUT OF THE BED,
AND RAN TO THE WINDOW

Goldilocks had pushed down the soft cushion in the middle-sized chair.

"SOMEBODY HAS BEEN SITTING
IN MY CHAIR!"

said the Middle-sized Bear, in his middle-sized voice.

And you know what Goldilocks had done to the third chair.

"SOMEBODY HAS BEEN SITTING IN MY
CHAIR AND HAS SAT THE BOTTOM
OUT OF IT!"

said the Little Small Wee Bear, in his little, small, wee voice.

Then the Three Bears thought that they had better search through the rest of the house, so they went upstairs into the bedchamber where they slept.

Now Goldilocks had pulled the pillow of the Great Big Bear out of its place, and he noticed it, first thing.

"SOMEBODY HAS BEEN
LYING IN MY BED!"

said the Great Big Bear, in his great, rough, gruff voice.

And Goldilocks had pulled the bolster of the Middle-sized Bear out of its place.

70

"SOMEBODY HAS BEEN LYING
IN MY BED!"
said the Middle-sized Bear, in his middle-sized voice.

And when the Little Small Wee Bear came to look at his bed, there was the bolster in its right place, and the pillow in its place upon the bolster, and upon the pillow was the golden-haired head of Goldilocks— which was not in its place, for she had no business there.

"SOMEBODY HAS BEEN LYING IN MY BED—
AND HERE SHE IS!"
said the Little Small Wee Bear, in his little, small, wee voice.

Now Goldilocks had heard in her sleep the great, rough, gruff voice of the Great Big Bear, but she was so fast asleep that it was no more to her than the roaring of the wind or the rumbling of thunder.

And she had heard the middle-sized voice of the Middle-sized Bear, but it was only as if she had heard someone speaking in a dream.

But when she heard the little, small, wee voice of the Little Small Wee Bear, it was so sharp and so shrill that it awakened her at once.

Up she started, and when she saw the Three Bears on one side of the bed, she tumbled herself out of the other side and ran to the window.

Now the window was wide open, because the Bears, like the good tidy Bears they were, always slept with their bedchamber window open. So out of the window jumped Goldilocks, and away she ran into the woods.

And whether or not she ever found her way out of the woods and became a better little girl, no one has ever known.

But the Three Bears never saw anything more of her.

JACK AND THE BEANSTALK

Once upon a time there was a poor widow who had an only son, named Jack. He was good-natured and affectionate but very lazy. As time went on, the widow grew poorer and poorer until she had nothing left in the world but her cow. And all the time, it seemed, Jack grew lazier and lazier.

One day Jack's mother said to him: "Tomorrow you must take the cow to market. And the more money you get for her the better for us, for we have nothing left to live on."

Next morning Jack got up earlier than usual, hung a horn around his neck, and started out with the cow. He was very happy at having such an important errand. On the way to market he met a queer little old man.

"Good-morning, my lad," said the queer little old man. "And where may you be going with that fine cow?"

"To market," replied Jack.

"And what may you be going to market for?" asked the queer little old man.

"To sell the cow," said Jack.

"As if you had wit enough to sell cows!" chuckled the queer little old man. "A lout of a lad that doesn't even know how many beans make five!"

"Two in each hand and one in your mouth," answered Jack, with a quickness that would have made his mother proud of him.

"Oho!" laughed the queer little old man. "Oho! Since you know beans, suppose you look at these," and he held out his hand, filled with sunrise-colored, sunset-colored, rainbow-colored beans. "I'll give you all these for your cow."

"That would be a good bargain," thought Jack; so he traded the cow for the beans, and hurried home to his mother. He could hardly wait to turn his pocket inside out and show her the treasure he had brought.

"Look," he said gleefully, as he poured the beans into her lap, "I got all these pretty beans for that one cow."

"You stupid boy," cried his mother angrily. "Now we shall have to starve." And she flung the beans out of the open window.

There was no supper for Jack that night, and the next morning he woke early, feeling very hungry. But why was his room so dark? And what was that shadow across his window? Jack jumped out of bed and went to the window to find out. It seemed as if a tall tree grew where no tree had been before.

Jack ran into the garden and found that it was not a tree but a beanstalk! And such a beanstalk! It had sprung up during the night from the beans his mother had thrown out of the window, and had grown so quickly its top was out of sight.

Jack began to climb, and he climbed and he climbed and he climbed. All the time he grew hungrier and hungrier and hungrier. It was almost noon when he reached the top of the beanstalk and stepped off into the sky where all the grass is blue. There was not a person or a house or a tree in sight. Jack walked on and on and on until he met a beautiful woman with a face like a star. She was dressed in shining clothes, and she carried a wand on the top of which was a little gold peacock.

"Good-morning, Jack," was her greeting.

"How in the world does she know my name?" thought Jack to himself, but he only said, taking off his cap: "Good-morning, my lady."

Now the lady was a fairy and she knew what Jack was thinking, and answered him without his having to ask any questions.

"I know who you are," she said, "and where you come from, and how you got here. And I will tell you where you are and what you are to do."

Then she told Jack he was in a country that belonged to a wicked Giant. This Giant had killed Jack's father and stolen all his gold and precious things. Jack had been only a baby at that time and could not remember, and his mother had been too sad even to talk to him about it. But that was why she was poor.

"If you and your mother are ever to be happy again," said the fairy, "you must punish that Giant. It will not be an easy thing to do, but you will succeed if you are brave."

The fairy whispered in Jack's ear for a minute, telling him what to do. Then she left him and Jack walked on and on and on.

Toward evening he came to the door of a castle. He blew his horn, and a woman as broad as she was tall, opened the door. "I am very tired and hungry," said Jack politely. "Can you give me supper and a night's lodging?"

"You little know, my poor lad, what you ask," sighed the square woman. "My husband is a giant, and eats people. He would be sure to find you and eat you for his supper. No, no, it would never do!" And she shut the door.

But Jack was too tired to go another step, so he blew his horn again, and when the Giant's wife came to the door he begged her to let him in. The Giant's wife began to cry, but at last she led Jack softly into the castle. She took him past dungeons where men and women were waiting to be killed. Then they came to the kitchen, and soon Jack was enjoying a good meal and quite forgetting to be afraid. But before he had finished there came a thump, thump, thump of heavy feet, and in less than no time

the Giant's wife had popped Jack into the great oven to hide.

The Giant walked in sniffing the air. "I smell boy," he thundered.

"You are dreaming," laughed his wife, "but there is something better than dreams in this dish." So the Giant stopped sniffing and sat down to supper.

Through a hole in the oven Jack peeped out and watched the giant eat. And how he did gobble! It seemed to Jack that no one, not even a giant, could possibly eat so much. When all the dishes were empty, the Giant bade his wife: "Bring me my hen."

She brought a much-ruffled hen and put it on the table.

"Lay," shouted the Giant, and the hen laid a golden egg.

"Another," roared the Giant, and the hen, though she had not done cackling over the first, laid another golden egg.

Again and again the Giant shouted his orders in a voice of thunder, and again and again the hen obeyed, till there were twelve golden eggs on the table. Then the Giant went to sleep, and snored so loud that the house shook.

When the biggest snore of all had shaken Jack out of the oven, he seized the hen and ran off as fast as he could. On and on and on he ran, until he reached the top of the beanstalk. He climbed quickly down, and carried the wonderful

hen, still cackling, to his mother. Day after day the hen laid its golden eggs, and by selling them Jack and his mother might have lived in luxury all their lives.

But Jack kept thinking about that wicked giant who had killed his father, and of the fairy's command. So one day he climbed the beanstalk again. When he reached the top he stepped off, followed the same path as before, and arrived at the Giant's castle. This time he had dressed himself to look like a very different person, as he did not want the Giant's wife to know him. And sure enough, when the square woman came to the door she did not recognize the lad she had hidden in the oven.

"Please," said Jack, "can you give me food and a place to rest? I am hungry and tired."

"You can't get in here," answered the Giant's wife. "Once before I took in a tired and hungry young runaway, and he stole my husband's precious hen that lays golden eggs."

But Jack talked to the Giant's wife so pleasantly that she thought it would be unkind to grudge him a meal. So she let him come in. After Jack had had a good supper the Giant's wife hid him in a big cupboard. And it was none too soon, either, for in stalked the Giant,

76

thump, thump, thump, sniffing the air. "I smell boy," he bellowed.

"Stuff and nonsense," said his wife, as she placed his supper on the table.

After supper the Giant roared· "Fetch me my money-bags."

His wife brought two heavy bags, one full of silver and one full of gold; and Jack, peeping out of the cupboard, said to himself: "Those were my father's money-bags." The Giant emptied the money out of the bags, counted it over and over again, and then put it back. Very soon he was fast asleep.

As soon as Jack heard the Giant's loud snores he stole out of the cupboard, snatched up the bags, and ran off as fast as he could. On and on he ran until he reached the top of the beanstalk. Then he dropped the money-bags into his mother's garden and climbed quickly down the beanstalk after them.

Jack and his mother were now as rich as the King and Queen, yet Jack felt that the Giant had not been punished enough yet. But it was some time before he dared climb again to the land at the top of the beanstalk.

At last, however, Jack made up his mind to disguise himself like a chimney sweep and see if he could persuade the Giant's wife to let him in

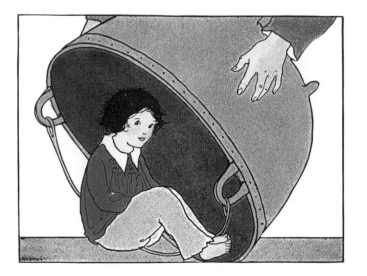

"Play!" commanded the Giant, and the harp began to play all by itself. Such lovely tunes Jack had never heard. It played and played until it played the Giant to sleep, and his snores drowned the sweet music. Then Jack jumped out from under the kettle, no blacker than he was himself, and seized the harp. But no sooner had he slung it up over his shoulder than it cried out: "Master, Master!" For it was a fairy harp.

Jack was frightened and ran for his life toward the top of the bean-stalk. He could hear the Giant running behind him, thump, thump, thump, but the Giant was so heavy he could not run very fast. Jack reached the top of the beanstalk and slid down it as quick as lightning, calling out as he went: "Mother. Mother! The axe, the axe!"

Jack's mother, holding out the axe, met him as he touched the ground. There was no time to lose, for the Giant was already half way down the beanstalk. It swayed and bowed under his weight. With one slashing blow Jack cut the beanstalk in two. There was a crash, and the Giant lay dead in the garden. Then Jack told his mother all the story, while the harp played a dirge for its old master. As for the won-derful beanstalk, it never grew again.

once more. He climbed the bean-stalk, followed the same path, and came to the castle door. The square woman did not know him, and he begged her for a night's lodging.

"No, no, no," she said, "you can't come in here. The last little beg-gars I took in were thieves. One stole the hen that laid the golden eggs, and the other stole the money-bags. No, no, you can't come in."

But Jack begged and begged, and at last the Giant's wife took pity on him, gave him his supper, and then turned over an empty kettle and hid him under it. Soon the Giant thumped in, sniffing the air, and roared out: "I smell boy."

"Boy?" laughed his wife. "You are always smelling boy." And she placed his supper on the table.

After supper the Giant shouted: "Fetch me my harp." And his wife brought in a beautiful harp with strings of pure gold.

HOW THE SEA BECAME SALT

Once upon a time, long, long, ago, there were two brothers, one of whom was rich and the other very poor. One cold Christmas Eve the poor brother found that he had not a thing in his house to eat, not even a morsel of bread or of meat, so he went to his rich brother and asked for a little food for his Christmas dinner.

The rich brother had helped him a few times before, but he had never felt glad to do so, for he was a very stingy man, in spite of his riches.

"If you'll do what I tell you, I will give you a whole ham for your Christmas dinner," he said.

"I must have food," said the poor brother. "So, if you will give me the ham, I promise to do whatever you tell me to do."

"Very well," said the rich brother, and threw the ham across to him. "And now go to the End of the Earth, for I am tired of having you always at my heels, asking me for food to eat or clothes to wear."

"Well, what I have promised I must keep," said the other one. "I don't know where the End of the

Earth is to be found, but perhaps I can ask some one along the way who can tell me." And so he took the ham under his arm and set out, and his rich brother was very glad to see him go.

The poor brother walked and walked the whole day, through the snow and the cold, and as it was growing dark he came to a place where the lights were shining brightly. "Perhaps this is the End of the Earth," he said to himself.

So he walked nearer to where the lights were shining, and there he came upon a very old man with a long white beard, cutting firewood for Christmas.

"Good evening," said the poor brother.

"Good evening to you," said the old man. "Where are you going this cold Christmas Eve?"

"I am going to the End of the Earth—that is to say, if I am on the right way," answered the poor brother.

"Yes, you are on the right way," said the old man. "There, where the lights are burning so brightly, is the walled castle which marks the

End of the Earth. When you get into the castle, everyone there will want to buy the ham which I see under your arm, for ham is scarce food in this land."

"Well, in that case," said the poor brother, "I shall sell my ham to them for ten gold pieces, and I shall be poor no longer."

"No, no!" cried the old man. "Do not sell your ham for gold or for jewels, no matter what they may offer you. Do not sell it unless they give you the magic hand-mill which stands just behind the door. When you come out again, I will show you how to use the mill, for it will be of great use to you in many ways."

"Very well," said the poor brother, and thanked the old man for his advice. Then he walked on toward where the lights were shining so brightly, and at last he came to the walled castle and knocked at the door in the wall.

And as soon as he was inside the castle, everyone there began to smell the delicious ham which he was carrying, and they all came running to buy it from him. Soon there was a great crowd around him, and lords and ladies were offering him gold and jewels for his ham.

At last the lord of the castle became angry, and cried out: "If

THE OLD MAN CUTTING HIS CHRISTMAS FIREWOOD

gold does not tempt you, is there anything else you will take for your ham? Come, speak up, my good man, for I want your ham for my Christmas dinner!"

"Well," said the poor brother, "my wife and I were going to have it for our own Christmas dinner, but since you want it so badly, I will let you have it. But if I am going to part with it, I must have the magic hand-mill which stands behind the door."

The lord did not like to part with the magic hand-mill, and he higgled and haggled with the poor brother, trying to persuade him to take something else. But the poor brother stuck to what he had said, and at last he got what he had asked for.

When at last he came out of the castle at the End of the Earth, he carried the hand-mill with him. He looked about for the old woodcutter, and when he had found him, the old man showed him how to use the magic mill.

It took him so long to learn all the old man had to tell him about the mill, that it was late before he got started homeward again, and he didn't get home until after the clock struck twelve on Christmas Day.

"Where in all the world have you been?" asked his wife. "Here

THE POOR BROTHER SHOWED HIS WIFE
THE MAGIC MILL

I have been waiting and waiting for hours, hoping that you would bring something for our Christmas dinner. And now all that you bring is that old hand-mill under your arm."

"It is a very wonderful mill," said her husband, "and I have been to the End of the Earth to get it. Just watch," and he set the mill in the middle of the bare table.

"Grind, mill, grind!" said he. "Grind food and good cheer for our Christmas dinner!"

And before he finished speaking, the magic mill began to grind, and it ground out first a fine tablecloth, and then plates and knives and forks, and last of all many delicious things to eat until the poor brother and his wife saw before them the most wonderful dinner they had ever dreamed of.

"What a wonderful mill!" cried the woman. "Will it grind anything you ask for?"

"It is a magic mill, and must be used carefully," said her husband. "But it will grind out all that we need to make us happy."

So the poor brother and his wife used the magic hand-mill carefully, and it ground out for them all the things they wished for to make them happy and comfortable. And at last the poor brother was the poor brother

THE MAGIC MILL GROUND OUT A WONDERFUL CHRISTMAS DINNER FOR THE POOR BROTHER AND HIS WIFE

no longer, but had become richer than his rich brother.

As for the rich brother, he became very angry when he saw that his poor brother was now richer than he, for he hated to see anyone prosper but himself.

"Where can he have found such wealth?" he wondered angrily. "On Christmas Eve he was so poor that I had to give him a ham, and now he is rich. I shall go at once and ask him where he got all the fine things he has."

So the rich brother went to the poor brother's house to see what he could find out.

"Ah, welcome," cried the poor brother, when he came to the door. "Now you shall see what a wonderful thing you did for me. You gave me a ham, and sent me to the End of the Earth. There I traded the ham for this magic hand-mill which you see here, and it has given me more riches than I ever dreamed of. And now, if you like, you shall see how it works."

THE RICH BROTHER GLEEFULLY CARRIED AWAY
THE MAGIC MILL

And he called on the mill to grind out rich food and gold pieces and many other things.

When the rich brother saw what a wonderful mill the magic hand-mill was, he was determined to have it at any cost. He offered many things, and each time he offered more, until at last its owner agreed to sell it for a thousand dollars.

"For," said the brother who had been poor, "I now have all the riches I want, so I do not need the mill any longer."

The rich brother carried the mill away in great glee, and he was so anxious to start it grinding things

for himself that he could hardly wait until he got home. When at last he got into the house he shut the doors, set the mill on the table, and thought of what he would have it grind out first.

"I shall grind out gold and other riches later on," he said. "To start with, I shall just try it out by making it grind something to eat."

So he turned to the mill and said: "Grind, mill, grind! Grind herrings and broth, and do it quickly and well!"

And before he finished speaking, the mill began to grind as hard as ever it could, and broth squirted out of one side in a great stream and herrings shot out of the other side by the dozens and hundreds!

A GREAT STREAM OF BROTH AND HERRINGS SHOT OUT

"Stop, mill, stop!" shouted the rich brother, for the broth from the mill had filled all the dishes and tubs in the house, and the herrings were piling up in a great heap.

But the mill would not stop, but kept on grinding out herrings and broth until the house was flooded, and if the doors had not given way and let the broth run out, the rich brother would perhaps have been drowned in it. When the doors tumbled down, the broth ran out of the house in great streams, washing the herrings and the rich brother together out through the yard and into the roadway!

As quickly as he could, the rich brother ran to his brother who had been poor, and shouted: "Come and stop the mill! If it grinds broth much longer, the whole town will be flooded and we shall all be drowned!"

So the poor brother agreed, for another thousand dollars, to stop the mill from grinding, and to take it back. He waded through the great stream of broth and herrings, and when at last he came to the mill he stopped its grinding at once. Then he tucked it under his arm and carried it back home with him.

The fame of the magic hand-mill spread far and wide, and many people came to see it grind. One day a

A SEA CAPTAIN COMES TO SEE THE MAGIC MILL

sea captain anchored his ship near by, and came to the fine house of the brother who had once been poor. "I have come to see your magic mill that grinds out whatever one asks for," he said. "I want to see if it will grind out salt."

"Salt?" said the owner of the mill. "Why do you wish it to grind salt?"

"I sail far away, across the ocean, to fill my ship with salt and bring it back to this land," said the captain. "If your mill will grind out salt, I will buy it from you, for it will fill my ship with salt in a much easier fashion than sailing across the ocean."

84

"Yes, it will grind salt," said the brother who had been poor. "But I am not sure that I want to sell the mill."

But the sea captain was determined to get the magic hand-mill, whatever the price, and finally he bought it for many thousands of dollars. He hurried back to his ship with it, and sailed away at once.

He was out to sea before he had a chance to start the mill grinding. At last he had it brought up on deck, and had piles of sacks placed near, so that none of the salt should be wasted, and then he started the mill to grinding.

"Grind, mill, grind!" he cried. "Grind salt, and grind it well! Salt! Salt! Nothing but salt!"

And before he had finished speaking, the mill began to grind salt at a great rate. It ground out salt so fast that the white streams of it spurted out at all sides.

At last all the sacks were filled with salt, and the ship was heavily loaded. And then the captain tried to stop the mill.

"Stop, mill, stop!" he cried, but the mill kept on grinding out more salt than ever. The white salt piled up on the deck higher and higher, no matter how hard the captain shouted for the mill to stop. At last the salt piled so high that it got into the captain's mouth, and he couldn't shout any more. And still the mill kept on grinding!

And finally, the salt became so heavy upon the deck of the ship that the ship sank, and down, down it went, to the bottom of the sea. And down, down went the mill also, still grinding, and there it is to this very day, still grinding salt. And that is how the sea became salt.

"NOW FLOPSEY, MOPSEY, COTTON-TAIL AND PETER, DON'T GET INTO MISCHIEF," SAID MRS. RABBIT

PETER RABBIT

Once upon a time there were four little rabbits, and their names were

Flopsey,

    Mopsey,

        Cotton-tail,

            and Peter.

They lived with their mother in a sand bank, underneath the root of a very big fir tree.

"Now, my dears," said old Mrs. Rabbit one morning, "you may go into the fields or down the lane, but don't go into Mr. McGregor's garden. Your father had an accident there; he was put into a pie by Mrs. McGregor.

"Now run along, and don't get into mischief. I am going out."

Then old Mrs. Rabbit took a basket and her umbrella, and went to the baker's. She bought a loaf of brown bread and five currant buns.

Flopsey, Mopsey, and Cotton-tail, who were good little bunnies, went down the lane to gather blackberries.

But Peter, who was very naughty, ran straight away to Mr. McGregor's garden, and squeezed under the gate!

First he ate some lettuce, and some French beans, and then he ate some radishes.

And then, feeling rather sick, he went to look for some parsley.

But round the end of a cucumber frame, whom should he meet but Mr. McGregor!

Mr. McGregor was on his hands and knees planting out young cabbages, but he jumped up and ran after Peter, waving a rake and calling out, "Stop, thief!"

Peter was most dreadfully frightened. He rushed all over the garden, for he had forgotten the way back to the gate.

He lost one of his shoes among the cabbages, and the other shoe among the potatoes.

After losing them, he ran on four legs and went faster, so that I think he might have got away altogether if he had not unfortunately run into a gooseberry net, and got caught by the large buttons on his jacket. It was a blue jacket with brass buttons, quite new.

Peter gave himself up for lost, and shed big tears; but his sobs were overheard by some friendly sparrows, who flew over him in great excitement, and begged him not to give up hope.

Mr. McGregor came up with a sieve, which he intended to pop upon the top of Peter Rabbit. But Peter wriggled out just in time, leaving his jacket behind him, and rushed into the tool shed, and jumped into a can.

It would have been a beautiful thing to hide in, if it had not had so much water in it.

Mr. McGregor was quite sure that Peter was somewhere in the tool shed, perhaps hidden underneath a flower-pot. He began to turn them over carefully, looking under each one. Presently Peter sneezed—"Ker-tchoo!"

Mr. McGregor was after him in no time, and tried to put his foot

PETER UPSET THREE PLANTS, JUMPING OUT A WINDOW

upon Peter, who jumped out of a window, upsetting three plants. The window was much too small for Mr. McGregor, and he was tired of running after Peter, anyway.

He went back to work.

Peter sat down to rest. He was out of breath and trembling with fright, and he had not the least idea which way to go. Also, he was very damp from sitting in that can.

After a time he began to wander about, going lippity—lippity—not very fast, and looking all around.

He found a door in a wall; but it was locked, and there was no room for a fat little rabbit to squeeze underneath.

An old mouse was running in and out over the stone doorstep, carrying peas and beans to her family in the wood. Peter asked her the way to the gate, but she had such a large pea in her mouth that she could not answer. So she shook her head at him. Peter began to cry.

Then he tried to find his way straight across the garden, but he became more and more puzzled.

Presently he came to a pond where Mr. McGregor filled his water cans. A white cat was staring at some goldfish; she sat very, very still, but now and then the tip of her tail twitched as if it were alive. Peter thought it best to go away without

88

speaking to her; he had heard about cats from his cousin, little Benjamin Bunny.

He went back toward the tool shed, but suddenly, quite close to him, he heard the noise of a hoe— scr-r-ritch, scratch, scratch, scritch. Peter scuttled underneath the bushes. But presently, as nothing happened, he came out, and climbed upon a wheelbarrow, and peeped over. The first thing he saw was Mr. McGregor hoeing onions. His back was turned toward Peter, and beyond him was the gate!

Peter got down very quietly off the wheelbarrow, and started running as fast as he could run along a walk behind some black-currant bushes.

Mr. McGregor caught sight of him at the corner, but Peter did not care. He slipped underneath the gate, and was safe at last in the wood outside the garden.

Mr. McGregor hung up the little jacket and the shoes for a scarecrow to frighten the blackbirds.

Peter never stopped running nor looked behind him until he got home to the big fir tree.

He was so tired that he flopped down upon the nice soft sand on the floor of the rabbit hole, and shut his eyes.

Mother Rabbit was busy cooking. She wondered what Peter had done

MOTHER RABBIT PUTS PETER TO BED

with his clothes. It was the second little jacket and the second pair of shoes that he had lost in a fortnight!

I am sorry to say that naughty Peter Rabbit was not very well during the evening.

His mother put him to bed, and made some camomile tea; and she gave a dose of it to Peter!

"One tablespoonful
            to be taken
                        at bedtime."
But Flopsey,
        Mopsey,
                and Cotton-tail
had bread and milk and blackberries for supper.

89

THE GINGERBREAD MAN RUNS AWAY

THE GINGERBREAD MAN

Once upon a time a little old man and a little old woman lived in a pleasant cottage around which ran a little white fence. The little old woman and the little old man were very happy, for their grandchildren lived near by.

Nearly every day the little girls and boys came over to see their grandparents, to keep them from getting lonely.

One day the little old woman was baking, and the little old man was hoeing out in the garden. When the little old woman had put her loaves of bread into the hot oven, she said to herself, "Now I shall make some gingerbread cookies for my little grandchildren to eat when they come to see me."

So she made some very fine gingerbread dough, and rolled it out very carefully, and cut a lot of gingerbread cookies with her cooky cutter. Then she put the cookies into a pan, and put the pan in the oven to bake.

"I have a lot of gingerbread dough left," she said to herself. "Now what shall I do with it?" So she thought about what she would do with the gingerbread dough that was left.

"I know what I'll do with the gingerbread dough," she said at last. "I shall make a little Gingerbread Man for my grandchildren." So she rolled out the dough again with great care, and very cleverly she shaped a little Gingerbread Man.

"Ah, doesn't he look fine?" she said at last. And indeed he did. He had a round little body, and a round little head, and two strong arms and two sturdy legs.

"And now to dress him up," said the little old woman, and she started making his clothes. She sprinkled brown sugar over his round little body to give him a little brown coat, and she stuck six big raisins in front for buttons. Then she gave him a pair of raisins for eyes, and a little lump of gingerbread for a nose. His mouth she made with some pink sugar which had been left over when she had last made a cake.

She was well pleased with him now, and she said:

"Ah, there, my little Gingerbread Man,
Now you're all ready to go to the pan."

"NO ONE SHALL EAT ME," CRIED THE GINGERBREAD MAN

So in the pan she laid him, and as soon as the bread and cookies were baked she popped him into the oven where they had been. Then she went on about her work while the fire burned and the oven baked the little Gingerbread Man.

At last the little old woman opened the oven door again.

"My little Gingerbread Man should be baked by this time," she said, and out of the oven she pulled the pan.

"My goodness, what a fine little Gingerbread Man he is," cried the little old woman when she saw what a wonderful brown color the hot oven had given him.

"I'll just lay him up in the cupboard to cool, and when my little grandchildren come to see me, they can eat him."

And then, what do you think happened?

The little Gingerbread Man, when he heard her say "eat him," jumped up in the shiny pan and hopped right out onto the clean white floor of the kitchen.

"No one shall eat me!" he cried, and ran toward the kitchen door on his sturdy little legs, shouting:

"I can run away from you, I can,
'Cause I'm the little Gingerbread
   Man!"

My goodness! but the little old woman was so surprised she didn't know what to do.

"Stop! Stop!" she called, just as he ran out of the door. "You are for my little grandchildren!" But the little Gingerbread Man wouldn't stop.

He ran on out into the yard, and through the garden toward the gate in the little white fence.

Out in the garden the little old man was hoeing, and when he saw the little Gingerbread Man running away, he dropped his hoe and ran after him.

"Stop! Stop!" cried the little old man, but the little Gingerbread Man wouldn't stop.

He darted out through the gate in the little white fence, shouting at the top of his voice:

"I can run away from you, I can.
  You can't catch me,
  'Cause I'm the little Gingerbread Man!"

And he ran down the road so fast that the little old man was left far behind.

On and on he ran, and after a while he ran past a farmyard where stood a big threshing machine, and where a crowd of men were threshing wheat. The threshers saw the little Gingerbread Man running past them, and they ran out and tried to stop him.

"Stop! Stop!" they cried, but the little Gingerbread Man wouldn't stop.

"Ha, ha, ha!" he laughed, as he dodged between their legs and ran on. And as he ran, he shouted back at them:

"I can run away from you, I can.
  I ran from the little old woman,
  And the little old man;
  And *you* can't catch me,
  'Cause I'm the little Gingerbread Man!"

On and on he ran, and after a while he met a big black dog.

"Stop! Stop!" cried the big black dog. "Stop, little Gingerbread Man, and I'll take you home for my puppies to play with!"

"STOP, GINGERBREAD MAN!" CRIED THE BIG BLACK DOG

But the little Gingerbread Man just laughed at the big black dog, and called back to her:

"I can run away from you, I can.
  I ran from the little old woman,
  And the little old man,
  And a yard full of threshers;
  And *you* can't catch me,
  'Cause I'm the little Gingerbread Man!"

Nor could the big black dog catch him, either, though she ran after him until she was tired.

After a while the little Gingerbread Man ran past a big yellow cow. "Stop! Stop!" cried the cow. "Stop, little Gingerbread Man, and let my little calf play with you!"

93

THE GINGERBREAD MAN LAUGHED AT THE BIG
YELLOW COW AND RAN ON

But the little Gingerbread Man just laughed at the big yellow cow, and called back to her, "If you can catch me, I'll stop and play with your little calf." The big cow, however, was too wise to run after him, and soon he had left her far behind.

After a while the little Gingerbread Man ran past a big tall horse. The big tall horse saw the little Gingerbread Man running along the road, so he jumped the fence and ran along the road, too.

He ran so fast—rackety-rackety-rackety!—that he soon caught up with the little Gingerbread Man, who began to get frightened. He thought that surely the big tall horse wanted to catch him.

But the big tall horse just ran along beside him, and said:

"This is the best race I ever ran!
What a runner you are, little
Gingerbread Man!"

For the big tall horse didn't want to catch him at all, but just wanted to run a race with him. And after they had run a while together, the horse stopped and turned back, saying:

"Run along, run along,
Little Gingerbread Man,
But beware of the fox,
For he'll catch you if he can!"

So the little Gingerbread Man once more ran along alone, and he

THE GINGERBREAD MAN RAN A RACE WITH THE HORSE

thought of what a fine fellow the big tall horse was. And after a while the little Gingerbread Man ran around a turn in the road, and who should be sitting there but the fox!

"Good day to you, little Gingerbread Man," called the fox. "What a runner you are! You must be tired from running so much."

The little Gingerbread Man stopped. Now that he thought of it, his sturdy little gingerbread legs *were* getting tired from so much running. "Yes, I am a little tired," he said to the fox.

"Ah, this is a very good place to rest," the fox told him. "My house is quite near, and you can rest there, and eat dinner with me, too. Running must have made you hungry."

Now that he thought of it, the little Gingerbread Man *was* hungry.

"How kind you are, Mr. Fox," he said. "I *am* tired and hungry."

"Just follow me, then," smiled the fox, "and you will soon feel much better, after you have rested and eaten dinner." And the fox led the way toward his house, with the tired little Gingerbread Man following along at his heels.

"What a fine treat he will make for my little ones!" thought the fox to himself. "They will lick the sugar from his coat and pick out his raisin eyes and then gobble down

"WHAT A RUNNER YOU ARE!" CALLED THE FOX

his arms and legs and his little round body." But of course he didn't say a word of this out loud, and the little Gingerbread Man never thought of being eaten.

At last, when they were almost at the fox's house, a little bird in a treetop near by saw them coming along, and sang out:

"Run! run! little Gingerbread Man,
For the fox will eat you if he can!"

Then the little Gingerbread Man stopped in his tracks, and he thought of what the big tall horse had said to him. "If you want to eat me," he called out to the fox, "you will have to catch me first!" And away he ran, with the fox right after him.

But the little Gingerbread Man could run much faster than the fox, and as he ran he shouted back for the angry fox to hear:

"I can run away from you, I can.
 I ran away from the little old woman,
 And the little old man,
 And a yard full of threshers,
 And a big black dog,
 And a big yellow cow.
 As fast as the big tall horse I ran,
 And *you* can't catch me,
 'Cause I'm the little Gingerbread Man!"

He ran on and on, and left the angry fox far behind. Past the big tall horse he ran, and back past the big yellow cow, and past the big black dog, and past the yard full of threshers. Then, as he came near the cottage of the little old man and the little old woman he was very tired.

Just as he neared the gate in the little white fence, some little girls and boys came through it. They were the grandchildren of the little old man and the little old woman, and they had been to see their grandparents.

"Why, here's the little Gingerbread Man that Grandmother baked for us!" they cried. "Let's catch him!" and after him they ran.

The little Gingerbread Man was glad. "I'll be a good little Gingerbread Man, and let them catch me," he said to himself, and he ran very slowly. "These are the very children I was made for, and so they shall have me, after all."

So the little Gingerbread Man ran so slowly that the little girls and boys soon caught him, and then they ate him up to the very last crumb. Which was just the best fate that could have befallen the little Gingerbread Man, after all, don't you think?

THE LITTLE RED HEN

There once lived, in a big barn-yard, a Little Red Hen and her brood of little fluffy chicks. She had for neighbors a fat little Pig and a Duck and a Goose.

The fat little Pig spent all of his time eating and sleeping, and so every day he grew fatter and fatter.

The Duck and the Goose liked to play in the water, and all day long they had a wonderful time swimming about in the barnyard pond.

But the Little Red Hen had very little time for play or for sleep, for she had to work hard all the time taking care of her chicks and seeing to it that they got enough to eat.

One day the Little Red Hen found a few grains of wheat scattered about on the ground near the granary door.

"Cluck! cluck!" called the Little Red Hen, and all her little chicks came running.

The Duck and the Goose came running, too, thinking the Little Red Hen had found something to eat, but the Pig, being so fat and lazy, just waddled up slowly.

"Cluck! cluck!" said the Little Red Hen. "Just see what I have found! Just look at these grains of wheat!"

"Oh, is that all?" said the Duck in disgust. "What are a few grains of wheat to get excited over? I could swallow them all, and never know I had eaten them."

"I could, too," said the Goose.

"And I," grunted the little fat Pig.

"Oh, yes," agreed the little Red Hen, "I know that they are very few and very small. But we can plant them, and they will grow and make many, many times as many grains as you see here. And then there will be enough for us all, and after they are made into flour we can all have bread and cake and other good things."

But the Duck and the Goose and the fat little Pig only looked at the grains of wheat on the ground and saw that they were very, very few— hardly enough, they thought, to bother about.

"Now who will help me plant this wheat?" asked the Little Red Hen, as she started to pick up the

ALL THE LITTLE CHICKS CAME RUNNING

grains of wheat one by one and put them in her apron.

"Not I," quacked the Duck.

"Nor I," honked the Goose.

"Nor I," grunted the little fat Pig.

"I will plant the wheat myself, then," said the Little Red Hen, and she hurried away to find a good place to plant the wheat grains she had found.

She finally found a place that suited her, and there she scratched and scratched away until at last she had made a wonderful bed for all the little grains of wheat. She planted them, every one, and covered them over nicely with fresh, clean earth.

By that time it was evening, and the Little Red Hen was very tired. But she was also very happy to know that all the little wheat grains were planted.

The rain fell and the sun shone, and by and by all the little grains of wheat sprouted and pushed their bright green blades up through their blanket of earth.

The Little Red Hen was very happy to see the little blades of wheat, and she sang as she led her chicks about.

Under the bright sun the tiny green blades soon grew tall, and after a while they put on their bearded bonnets and began to droop their heavy heads. A little while longer, and they began to grow tired of their green garb and changed it to a golden hue.

The Little Red Hen had been keeping close watch upon them as they grew, and when she saw them all dressed in their golden holiday clothes she was very much pleased, indeed.

"The wheat is ripe, is ripe, is ripe!" she sang as she ran about the barnyard. "Now who will help me cut it?"

"Not I," quacked the Duck.

"Nor I," honked the Goose.

"Nor I," grunted the fat little Pig from his bed in the shade.

"Then I will cut it myself," declared the Little Red Hen, and she hurried into the barn for a sickle.

She worked long and hard that day, cutting the golden wheat and stacking it in little cocks so that the sun could dry it out and loosen the grains in the ears.

By the time she had finished it was evening, and the Little Red Hen was very tired, but she was also happier than ever to know that the wheat had all been cut.

But the wheat had to be threshed, and the Little Red Hen thought that her neighbors surely would help her this time.

"Who will help me thresh the wheat?" she called out one morning, bright and early.

"Not I," quacked the Duck.

"Nor I," honked the Goose.

"Nor I," grunted the little fat Pig.

"Dear me, then I guess I shall have to thresh it myself," said the Little Red Hen, and into the barn she ran to find a flail.

With the flail she beat all the golden grains from the ears, and by the time all the wheat was threshed and the chaff fanned away, it was evening.

The little Red Hen was very tired after all the hard work of the day, but she was also very happy to see such a nice big lot of wheat.

"WHY DO YOU CARRY SUCH A HEAVY LOAD?"
ASKED THE DUSTY MILLER

"Now," said she, bright and early the next morning, "the wheat has been planted and cut and threshed, and a fine heavy load of it there is. Who will help me carry it to the mill?"

"Not I," quacked the Duck.

"Nor I," honked the Goose.

"Nor I," grunted the fat little Pig.

"Well, in that case," said the Little Red Hen, "I will carry it to the mill myself," and away she ran into the barn to get a sack to carry the wheat in.

She filled the sack with the wheat, and threw it over her back. Then away she went toward the mill, stopping to rest every little bit along the way because the wheat was so heavy.

When at last the Little Red Hen came to the mill, there was the Dusty Miller himself standing in the doorway.

"Good day to you, Mr. Dusty Miller," said the Little Red Hen.

"And to you, good day, Little Red Hen," said the Dusty Miller. "Why do you carry such a heavy load?"

"It is wheat I bring to your mill, Mr. Dusty Miller," said the Little Red Hen. "I planted and reaped it, I threshed it and fanned the chaff away, and now I bring it to you to have it ground into flour."

And so the Dusty Miller lifted the big sack of wheat from the back of the Little Red Hen and carried it into his mill. There he poured it into a big hopper and started the millstones to turning.

It wasn't very long before all the grains of wheat the Little Red Hen had brought had been ground up by the Dusty Miller into soft white flour.

Then indeed was the Little Red Hen happy.

"Thank you, Mr. Dusty Miller," said she. "The wheat that I planted and reaped, threshed and carried to mill, is now soft white flour, and my little chicks will have fine bread and cake."

And she picked up her sack of flour which the Dusty Miller had ground, and hurried homeward.

"Who will help me bake the bread?" she called, when she had reached the barnyard once more.

"Not I," quacked the Duck.

"Nor I," honked the Goose.

"Nor I," grunted the fat little Pig.

"Then I will bake it myself," said the Little Red Hen, and she carried the sack of flour into her neat little house and began to make it into fine white bread.

When at last the bread was baked, and came out of the oven in fine big loaves, she set it carefully aside to cool and stepped to the door of her little house.

"Cluck! cluck!" she called, and all her little chicks came running.

The Duck and the Goose came running, too, thinking that she had something for them to eat.

And the lazy little fat Pig also came—so fast that he was all out of breath, for he had smelled the warm bread and his mouth watered for a taste of it.

"The wheat I planted and reaped, threshed and carried to mill," said the Little Red Hen, "is baked into fine white bread. Now who will help me eat it?"

"CLUCK! CLUCK!" CALLED THE LITTLE RED HEN, "NOW WHO WILL HELP ME EAT THIS FINE WHITE BREAD?"

"I will!" quacked the Duck, waddling close to the door.

"I will, too!" loudly honked the hungry Goose, stretching out her long neck.

"And I!" squealed the fat little Pig, very much awake at the thought of getting some of the fine fresh bread he had smelled.

"Ah, do you think so?" said the Little Red Hen. "I planted the wheat and reaped it, I threshed it and carried it to mill, I made the bread and baked it—and now you would help me eat it! No, indeed! Workers work that workers may eat, and when lazy folks shirk they must go hungry. Cluck! cluck! cluck!" and she called all her chicks into the house and shut the door tight.

The Duck and the Goose and the little fat Pig gazed hungrily through the windows at the Little Red Hen and her chicks eating a fine supper of fresh bread and other good things, and they began to feel very sorrowful.

"Oh, dear! Oh, dear!" quacked the Duck. "Why did I not help the Little Red Hen? Then I should have had fine white bread for my supper, too."

"What a lazy dunce I have been," hissed the Goose to herself. "I wouldn't work, and now I must go hungry."

"Oink! oink!" grunted the fat little Pig sadly. "A little work and a little less sleep wouldn't have hurt me any. Why, oh, why, didn't I help the Little Red Hen?"

But the Little Red Hen who had worked so hard was happy, and she sang as she cut thick slices of the fresh bread and spread them with butter and jam for her chicks.

THE PIED PIPER

Beside the broad River Weser there was once a rich and pleasant city named Hamelin. The people were happy and contented, and they thought Hamelin the finest city in the world.

Then, one day, a dreadful plague fell upon them, and they were happy no longer. An army of thousands and millions of rats descended upon the city, and soon the good people of Hamelin were so overrun with rats that they did not know what to do!

But the army of rats was having a most wonderful time:

They fought the dogs and killed the
  cats,
  And bit the babies in the cradles,
And ate the cheeses out of the vats,
  And licked the soup from the
  cooks' own ladles,
Split open the kegs of salted sprats,
Made nests inside men's Sunday hats,
And even spoiled the women's chats
  By drowning their speaking
  With shrieking and squeaking
In fifty different sharps and flats.

At last the people of Hamelin could stand the rats no longer. They all met together in the public square and marched to the Town Hall.

There they burst in on the Mayor and his Council.

"Rid us of the rats!" they cried to the Mayor and his Council. "Rouse up, sirs! Rack your brains, and find a way to rid us of the rats! For if you don't, and quickly, out of Hamelin you go forever, to beg for your bread on the highway!"

The Mayor and all his Councilmen were very much frightened. They shivered in their fine robes, and thought in vain for a way to get rid of the army of rats.

"I wish I were far away, and had never heard of a rat!" cried the Mayor. "I've racked my brain until it hurts, and still I can't think of a way to get rid of the rats."

"Traps are no good," said one Councilman. "They just use traps for toys."

"Cats are no good," said another Councilman. "They kill the cats."

"Dogs are no good," mourned a third Councilman. "They kill the dogs, too!"

"I would gladly give a thousand guilders to be rid of this plague of rats!" cried the Mayor, wiping his brow.

And just as he said it, there came a soft rapping at the door.

"Who can that be?" muttered the Councilmen, fearful that the towns-people had come back.

The Mayor was frightened, too, but he called out, "Come in!"

And into the Council Chamber and up to the Council Table stepped the queerest-looking stranger that had ever been seen in Hamelin:

His queer long coat from heel to
    head
Was half of yellow and half of
    red,
And he himself was tall and thin,
With sharp blue eyes, each like a
    pin,
And light loose hair, yet swarthy
    skin,
But lips where smiles went out
    and in.

"Please your honors," said he, "in many lands I am called the Pied Piper because of the colors which I wear and the pipe which I carry. I have a charm in my magic pipe, and I have come far to rid Hamelin of its rats."

The Mayor and his Council sat back in surprise, and stared at the queer stranger.

They noticed that there was a long scarf about his neck, and that at its end hung a pipe. They saw that his fingers strayed to it as he stood there, and touched it as

"I HAVE A CHARM IN MY MAGIC PIPE"
SAID THE PIED PIPER

though he were anxious to be making music upon it.

"With my magic pipe," he went on, "I can charm any living creature to follow me and do as I choose. I use my power mostly to charm away hurtful creatures that do people harm.

"In Tartary, last year, I piped away a huge swarm of gnats; in India, I piped away a cloud of vampire bats; and elsewhere I have piped away other plagues. So now with my magic pipe I have come to Hamelin to rid you of your rats."

"Fine! Splendid!" roared the Mayor and his Council.

"I heard you speak about a thousand guilders," said the Pied Piper. "Will you give me that if I pipe your rats away?"

"A thousand? It's worth fifty thousand!" cried the Mayor and his Council.

"Let it be just a thousand," smiled the Pied Piper. "Do you promise?"

"We promise!" roared the Mayor and his Council, gladly.

And, with another smile, the Pied Piper passed out through the door and stepped into the street.

Out in the street, he lifted his magic pipe to his lips and blew a few shrill notes—"Tootle-tee-too! tootle-ooo-oo!" Then he started piping in earnest, and as the sweet, strange notes came from his pipe, a most wonderful thing began to happen!

A murmur like the moving of an army, was heard above the music! The murmuring grew to a grumbling, and then the grumbling grew to a mighty rumbling, and from every direction the rats came tumbling!

They hurried from the houses and they scurried from the barns, and so many, many of them were there that they poured out into the alleys like streams of water. The streams poured into the street, and there all the rats ran together, and they flowed like a big river down the street toward the

Pied Piper! There were big rats and little rats, old rats and young rats, father rats and mother rats, brothers and sisters, uncles and aunts, grandparents and cousins—every rat in Hamelin!

And down the street the Pied Piper walked, and after him followed the rats. He walked until he came to the broad River Weser, which flowed beside the town, and there he stood and piped until all the rats had come near. Then he took his pipe from his lips and said to one of the leaders:

"Are they all here, Rat Prince?"

"Every rat in Hamelin is here, sir!" squeaked the Rat Prince.

"Very well," smiled the Pied Piper, and he began to pipe again.

And then what do you think happened?

As they heard the new notes the Piper played, all the rats—thousands and millions of them—ran as hard as they could toward the river and jumped right into its cold, swift water! And then, first thing anyone knew, there wasn't a rat left in Hamelin. They were all drowned!

That is, all were drowned but one. One rat escaped—he was the big gray rat that had first told the Rat King about Hamelin—and he alone

THEN AS THE PIED PIPER PLAYED, THE GREAT ARMY OF RATS RAN DOWN TO THE BROAD RIVER
AND JUMPED INTO ITS COLD SWIFT WATER

swam safely to the other side of the river. Then he hurried away to Ratland as fast as ever he could, and told the big Rat King of what had happened.

"At the first shrill notes of the pipe, we seemed to hear the sounds of rich food being put out for a mighty feast," said he. "We felt a great hunger, and rushed out in crowds. And the pipe seemed to say, 'Oh, rats, rejoice! The whole world is grown into one vast cupboard, where you may all eat the choicest food until you grow tired of it. Just follow—follow—follow—'

THE MAYOR AND THE COUNCILMEN THINKING OF HOW THEY MIGHT GET RID OF PAYING THE PIED PIPER

"So we followed the sound of the pipe as though a cheese were only an inch from our noses. And just as we were about to bite into the cheese—the River Weser rolled over us! And only I am left of all the mighty Rat Army!"

And the big gray rat shed tears of sorrow.

In Hamelin the Mayor and his Council were gathered together with some of the townspeople. They were planning a great feast to celebrate being rid of the rats. And as they were deciding about the wonderful feast they were going to have, there came a rapping at the door.

"Who can that be?" wondered the Councilmen.

"Come in!" cried the Mayor, and into the Council Chamber and up to the Council Table walked the Pied Piper.

"We are going to give a great feast to celebrate being rid of the rats," said the Mayor in a hearty voice. "And you, Pied Piper, may join us."

But the Pied Piper shook his head.

"I have other lands to visit and other plagues to pipe away with my magic pipe," he said. "I tarry just long enough to get the thousand guilders you promised me."

A thousand guilders! The Mayor looked blue, and the Councilmen looked blue, and the townpeople looked bluest of all. For if they gave the Pied Piper his thousand guilders, they couldn't buy the food for their wonderful feast.

So they all thought of how they might get rid of the Pied Piper without paying him what they had promised.

At last the Mayor winked to the others, and said to the Pied Piper: "Oh, that was just a little joke!" and all but the Pied Piper laughed. "Besides, the river really killed the rats, not you. With our own eyes we saw the river drown them. So, of course, we can't pay you for the work which our own good River Weser did."

And the Councilmen and the townspeople all nodded their heads and smiled, for they agreed with the Mayor.

But the Pied Piper only frowned darkly upon them.

"Come! come!" cried the Mayor. "We don't mind giving you fifty guilders, to make your journey easy. But as for a thousand guilders—that is out of the question!"

The Pied Piper's face grew hard and angry. "Your promise!" cried he. "I have no time for bargaining now. I must be off, and if you will not pay, you may make me pipe for you in a different fashion!"

ONCE MORE THE PIED PIPER PUT HIS PIPE
TO HIS LIPS

But the Mayor and his Council and the townspeople only laughed, and the Pied Piper walked angrily out of the door.

Out in the street once more, the Pied Piper put his magic pipe to his lips again.

At the first shrill notes, everyone came running to see why he was piping now, since there were no longer any rats.

And then they beheld a fearful sight! As the Piper piped, out of the houses came running all the children of the town, all the little girls and little boys in Hamelin!

108

ALL THE LITTLE BOYS AND GIRLS IN HAMELIN FOLLOWED THE PIED PIPER

They ran and danced after the Pied Piper, and followed him as he walked down the street.

The Mayor and his Council, and all the grown-up townspeople, tried to call out to their children to come back, but they found that they could not move or say a word! All they could do was to stand and watch their children follow the Piper out of the town!

Away went the Pied Piper, piping sweetly on his magic pipe, until at last he came to the River Weser. And the townspeople groaned to themselves, for they remembered what had happened to the rats there.

But when the Pied Piper came to the river he turned and walked along its bank, with all the little girls and boys following along behind him.

"He'll have to turn back when he gets to Koppelburg Hill!" thought the Mayor. And sure enough, right in the path of the Pied Piper and shutting off the way, was a huge hill so steep that no one could ever climb over it.

And so, anxiously, the Mayor and his Council and all the townspeople watched the Pied Piper and the children come nearer and nearer to Koppelburg Hill.

"He must stop now," said they all to themselves. "He surely can lead them no farther."

But when the Pied Piper came to the hill he did not stop. Instead, as he piped, a wondrous doorway opened wide before him, right in the steep side of the hill. And through it the Piper marched, still piping, and all the little children danced in after him. Then, when all were in the hill, the door closed, and there was no sign of it left!

Then it was that the Mayor and his people came to life again, and all rushed toward the hill to see if they could find their children. But never a sign of the magic doorway could they find, and though they searched long and hard, neither could they find their children.

The Mayor and the people of Hamelin were very sad because they had lost all their little girls and boys, and they began to feel sorry that they had cheated the Pied Piper. They sent word in every direction that they would pay him many times the thousand guilders if he would only bring their children back to them.

But whether the Pied Piper never got their message, or whether he got it and thought they were just

THE PIED PIPER MARCHED ON AND AFTER HIM DANCED THE HAPPY LITTLE CHILDREN

trying to cheat him again, no one ever knew.

For the people of Hamelin never saw the Pied Piper or their little boys and girls again.

As for the happy little children who had danced away and followed him into the hill, the Pied Piper led them far away to a wondrous and joyous land where they were always happy. There they grew up and lived to a fine old age with never a sorrow to trouble them. But their parents, who had tried to cheat the Pied Piper, never heard of them again.

MR. AND MRS. VINEGAR

Once, in a little green garden, there was a big glass pickle jar. And this big glass pickle jar was the home of a little old man and a little old woman whose names were Mr. and Mrs. Vinegar.

All day long Mr. Vinegar cared for his garden so that there would be plenty of vegetables for his wife to make into pickles.

As for Mrs. Vinegar, she was a very neat old body, always washing and scrubbing and cleaning — when she was not busy at her pickle making.

For, you see, since the pickle jar was made of glass, every little spot and speck of dust showed up very plainly on it.

One day when Mrs. Vinegar was sweeping her house, she saw a cobweb high up over her head. She tried to reach it with her broom, but it was too high. Then she tried standing on a chair, and when she stood on the chair her broom just reached the cobweb, but still she was not high enough to sweep it down.

Mrs. Vinegar tried and tried to sweep the cobweb down, and at last she lost her temper. And then she

swept so hard at it that — crack! crash! bang! — her broom hit the side of the pickle jar and smashed it all to smithereens!

"Oh, dear!" cried Mrs. Vinegar. "What have I done now?"

She picked her way out of the broken pickle jar and ran to where Mr. Vinegar was digging in his garden with a pickle fork.

"Oh, Vinegar, Vinegar!" she cried to her husband. "Whatever shall we do? I've smashed our pickle jar to smithereens!"

"Oh, have you, Lovey?" said Mr. Vinegar, and he threw down his pickle fork. "In that case, I need not till my vegetables any longer, for of what use are pickles without a pickle jar to put them in?"

But Mrs. Vinegar did not answer. She only sat down on a wheelbarrow and wept bitterly.

"Come, come!" cried Mr. Vinegar. "Accidents will happen. Besides, there are many other pickle jars just as good as ours was."

"But we have no money to buy one with," sobbed Mrs. Vinegar.

"Oh, that will be all right," said Mr. Vinegar. "We'll just go out

MRS. VINEGAR STOOD ON A CHAIR AND TRIED
TO SWEEP THE COBWEB DOWN

Vinegar carried the door to their pickle-jar house on his back.

They trudged along all day, seeking their fortune, but not a cent did they find.

As it began to get dark, they found themselves in the middle of a big woods, with not a house in sight.

"Oh, Vinegar, Vinegar!" cried Mrs. Vinegar. "Wherever shall we sleep tonight? We are in the middle of a big woods, where wild beasts will surely get us!" and she began to weep bitterly.

"Don't worry, my love," said Mr. Vinegar cheerfully. "I'll just fix

in the world and seek our fortune, and when we find it we can buy another pickle jar to live in."

So they decided to go out into the world to seek their fortune.

"But what will happen to all our furniture?" asked Mrs. Vinegar, when they were ready to start. "Someone may steal it."

"Oh, never fear," said Mr. Vinegar. "Can't you see that I'm taking the door to our house with us? If I have the door on my back, surely no one can open it and steal our furniture, can they?"

"Very true," said Mrs. Vinegar, and together they set out. Mrs. Vinegar carried their lunch, and Mr.

AS THEY SET OUT MR. VINEGAR CARRIED THE DOOR
TO THEIR HOUSE ON HIS BACK

112

MR. AND MRS. VINEGAR AND THEIR PICKLE-JAR HOME

the pickle-jar door up high in the crotch of a tall tree, and we can sleep there safe from all harm."

So he climbed a big tall tree, and fixed the door firmly in a fork of the limbs. Then he helped Mrs. Vinegar up the tree, and they both lay down on the door and went safely to sleep.

Just a little past midnight, Mr. Vinegar woke up. He thought he heard voices, and he listened closely. Sure enough, he could hear the sound of rough voices plainly, and he knew he was not dreaming. He looked down from his perch, and there — on the ground right below him — was a fire. And around the fire was clustered a band of fierce robbers, dividing a bag of gold they had stolen.

"Oo-o-ooh!" groaned Mr. Vinegar, and he was so frightened that he started trembling mightily.

"Keep still, Vinegar!" muttered Mrs. Vinegar, half asleep. "You're about to shake me out of bed!" Then she went to sleep again.

But Mr. Vinegar kept on shaking and trembling, and then — before he knew it — he shook the door right out of the tree! As the door fell, he caught on a limb and hung in the tree.

But the door, with Mrs. Vinegar sound asleep upon it, crashed down

ALL NIGHT MR. VINEGAR HUNG IN THE TREE
LIKE A FUNNY LITTLE MONKEY

to the ground right on top of the robbers. When the door fell on them the robbers thought the sky was falling, and ran away as fast as their legs could carry them!

And so soundly was Mrs. Vinegar sleeping that the crash of the falling door didn't wake her up at all!

All night Mr. Vinegar hung in the tree, like a funny little monkey. And when morning came he looked down and saw that the robbers were gone. Then he began to feel cheerful again, and he felt very brave as he remembered how he had scared the robbers away.

114

At last, as the sun grew brighter, Mrs. Vinegar sat up and rubbed her eyes and yawned.

"Why, where am I?" she cried, when she looked around.

"You are down on the ground, Lovey!" called out Mr. Vinegar, and he scrambled down from the tree to the ground and helped his wife to her feet.

Then they picked up the door, and guess what they found!

There was one of the robbers squashed flatter than a pancake, and there was a bag with forty pieces of gold in it!

"We have found our fortune!" cried Mr. and Mrs. Vinegar, and together they danced about for joy.

MR. AND MRS. VINEGAR DANCED ABOUT FOR JOY

"Now we can buy *two* pickle jars if we want them," said Mr. Vinegar. "And you, Lovey, can get back to your pickle making."

But quite suddenly Mrs. Vinegar felt tired of making pickles. "No, no, Vinegar," said she. "Let us try something else besides pickle making. Now that we have money, we can pick and choose. So let us buy a cow and run a dairy. The cow will give us milk and butter, which we can sell, and we shall fare well all the rest of our days."

"How wise you are, Wifey!" cried Mr. Vinegar in admiration.

"So go to market in the next town, Vinegar," Mrs. Vinegar went on, "and buy a good cow there. I'll wait for you here. And mind you don't pay too much for the cow."

"Very well, Lovey," said Mr. Vinegar, and away he went to buy a cow, jingling the gold pieces in his pocket.

And when he had come to the market he saw a man leading an old black cow along.

"That is the very cow for me!" said Mr. Vinegar to himself. "If I can buy that cow, I shall be the happiest man in the world!"

So he walked up to the man, and he clinked his gold pieces and said, "Do you wish to sell that cow, kind sir?"

"THIS IS A WONDERFUL COW!" SAID THE MAN AS HE HEARD THE JINGLE OF GOLD IN MR. VINEGAR'S POCKET

The man heard the jingle of gold pieces, and he saw that Mr. Vinegar was something of a simpleton. So he said, "This is a very wonderful cow! As you see, she is black. But when she eats green grass she gives white milk, and the white milk makes yellow butter! She is such a colorful cow that I wouldn't sell her for anything except what you have in your pocket!"

"Done!" cried Mr. Vinegar happily. So he handed over his forty gold pieces to the man and led the cow away.

But the black cow would not walk fast, and Mr. Vinegar tugged and pulled at the rope about her neck until he was tired. He sat down to rest, and while he was resting he saw a bagpiper.

The piper was marching up and down the street, piping away lustily, and such fine music did he make that everyone stopped to listen. And coins of all kinds were thrown into his hat every time he held it out.

"How wonderful it would be to have those bagpipes," Mr. Vinegar said to himself. "And how rich one

116

WHAT A DREADFUL SCREECHING AND SQUALLING
THE BAGPIPES DID MAKE!

So Mr. Vinegar hung the bagpipes over his shoulder, and the bagpiper walked away with the old black cow. And then Mr. Vinegar started to play the bagpipes!

Oh, me! Oh, my! What a dreadful screeching and squalling the pipes made as Mr. Vinegar tried to get them to play a tune! The children cried and ran out of the street, and the people all stuck their fingers in their ears!

And instead of tossing money to Mr. Vinegar for his playing, they threw clods and sticks at him.

But Mr. Vinegar kept on marching up and down the street as the bagpiper had done, and he kept on trying to play a tune until his fingers were almost frozen and he was all out of breath.

Then he saw a man with big fur gloves, and he thought of his almost frozen fingers.

"Ah, if I only had those gloves," he said to himself, "I should be the happiest man in the world!"

So he went to the man with the big fur gloves, and said to him: "What will you take for those gloves, kind sir?"

And the man, seeing the bagpipes, and seeing also that Mr. Vinegar was something of a simpleton, said to him, "Your hands are blue with cold and so, as a favor to you, I will

could become with all the money that is given to the piper. Ah, I should be the happiest man in the world if I only owned those bagpipes!"

So he went up to the bagpiper, and said, "What will you take for your bagpipes, kind sir?"

The musician saw the old black cow, and he saw that Mr. Vinegar was something of a simpleton, so he said, "Well, this is a wonderful instrument, and brings me a great deal of money. Nothing but that black cow you have would get me to part with it."

"Done!" cried Mr. Vinegar happily. "You may have the cow. Now give me the pipes!"

trade you my warm fur gloves for your bagpipes."

"Done!" cried Mr. Vinegar happily. He gave the man the bagpipes, and put on the fur gloves. And in a little while his hands were as warm as toast and he thought himself the happiest man in the world.

So away he went, trudging along the rough road back to where he had left Mrs. Vinegar. Then, presently, his feet began to hurt from the rough walking. And just as they began to hurt the worst, he saw a man with a stout staff.

"Oh, me! Oh, my!" said Mr. Vinegar to himself. "If I only had that staff to help me along the road, my feet wouldn't hurt so badly and I would be the happiest man in the world." So he said to the man with the staff, "What will you take for your staff, kind sir?"

The man, seeing that Mr. Vinegar was something of a simpleton, said to him, "You may have my staff for your warm fur gloves."

"Done!" cried Mr. Vinegar happily, and he gave the fur gloves for the staff.

Then he walked on cheerfully, using the staff to help him along the rough road. He thought of what a good bargain he had made, and that now he was the happiest man in the world.

"WHAT WILL YOU TAKE FOR YOUR STAFF, KIND SIR?"
ASKED MR. VINEGAR

And as he was walking along, a jaybird saw him and flew over him, laughing heartily.

"Ha-ha-ha!" the jaybird laughed. "Oh, how funny-funny-funny!"

"What are you laughing at, jaybird?" asked Mr. Vinegar. For if there was something funny to laugh at, he wanted to laugh too.

"I'm laughing at you!" cried the jaybird. "At *you*, Mr. Vinegar! You gave forty gold pieces for a cow that wasn't worth five—you traded the cow for bagpipes you couldn't play—you traded the pipes for a pair of gloves—and you traded the gloves for an old staff. So now all you have to show for your forty gold pieces is an old stick. Ha-ha-ha! Oh, Mr. Vinegar, what a dunce you are, to be sure! Ha-ha-ha! Ha-ha-ha! Oh, how funny-funny-funny!"

And the jaybird laughed and laughed until he could hardly fly!

At last Mr. Vinegar began to get angry, for he could see that the joke was really on him, and he didn't like that kind of a joke at all. He drew back his staff and hurled it as hard as he could at the jaybird.

But the staff missed the bird, and landed high in the top of a tall tree, where Mr. Vinegar couldn't get it. And then didn't the jaybird laugh!

"And *now* you have nothing!" he cried. "Oh my, what a simpleton you are, Mr. Vinegar! Ha-ha-ha!"

But Mr. Vinegar hurried along, wondering what Mrs. Vinegar would say when he came back to her with nothing at all to show for the forty gold pieces.

And when he told her all about it, my! my! but didn't she say plenty! Mr. Vinegar's ears burned for a week afterward! But when it was all over, they settled down cheerfully to decide what to do.

So Mr. Vinegar started working for a farmer, and Mrs. Vinegar helped the farmer's wife. And they saved the money they made, and by and by they bought another pickle jar to live in.

"And now, Lovey," said Mr. Vinegar, "here we are back to our garden and pickle making, doing the things we are best fitted to do."

And that ends the story of Mr. and Mrs. Vinegar.